"I'll have to go back to Bellport and talk to Ada.

"If what Katie says is true, then she's obviously not the right person to guide a teenage girl."

Dorcas bit her lip to keep from saying that Jacob should have realized that before and tried to look approving. At least he was doing it now.

"In the meantime, someone must look after Katie," he went on.

"Can't she stay with you?"

"And leave her alone all day?"

"She could stay here for a visit. I'd enjoy having her, and what would be more natural than for her to spend time with her mother's best friend?"

She could see the word *no* forming on his lips, but it didn't come out. Instead, he let out a long breath.

He cleared his throat. "Would you be kind enough to have Katie here for a visit?"

"For sure. We'd love it."

"*Denke.*" He put his hand over hers for a brief moment. "You're a good friend for her, Dorcas."

Was she a friend to him, as well? She doubted he could see her that way, but at least she'd moved a step forward.

A lifetime spent in rural Pennsylvania and her Pennsylvania Dutch heritage led **Marta Perry** to write about the Plain People who add so much richness to her home state. Marta has seen over seventy of her books published, with over seven million books in print. She and her husband live in a beautiful central Pennsylvania valley noted for its farms and orchards. When she's not writing, she's reading, traveling, baking or enjoying her six beautiful grandchildren.

Books by Marta Perry

Love Inspired

Brides of Lost Creek

Second Chance Amish Bride
The Wedding Quilt Bride
The Promised Amish Bride
The Amish Widow's Heart
A Secret Amish Crush
Nursing Her Amish Neighbor
The Widow's Bachelor Bargain

An Amish Family Christmas
"Heart of Christmas"
Amish Christmas Blessings
"The Midwife's Christmas Surprise"

Visit the Author Profile page
at LoveInspired.com for more titles.

The Widow's Bachelor Bargain

Marta Perry

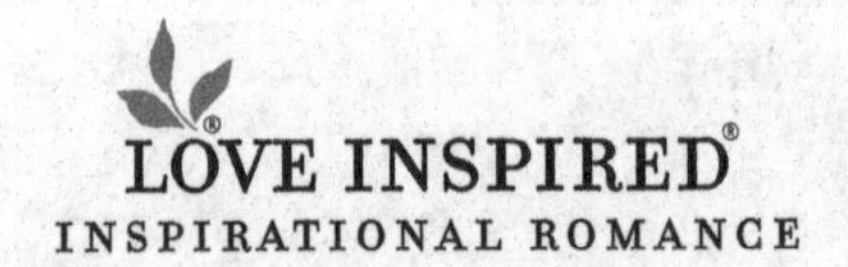

ISBN-13: 978-1-335-41776-3

The Widow's Bachelor Bargain

For questions and comments about the quality of this book, please contact us at CustomerService@Harlequin.com.

Love Inspired
22 Adelaide St. West, 41st Floor
Toronto, Ontario M5H 4E3, Canada
www.LoveInspired.com

Printed in U.S.A.

And let us not be weary in well doing:
for in due season we shall reap, if we faint not.
As we have therefore opportunity,
let us do good unto all men, especially unto
them who are of the household of faith.

—*Galatians* 6:9–10

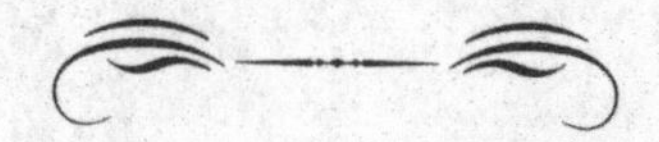

This story is dedicated to my husband with love and thanks for sixty-two wonderful years.

Chapter One

Dorcas Bitler turned the buggy toward home while she stared at her ten-year-old son in dismay. She certainly hadn't expected to be confronted with a challenge like this from the Englisch world so early in Timothy's life. For a moment her heart yearned to have Luke there… Luke with his loving smile and his ability to steer his sons in the right direction with no more than a word or a laugh.

But Luke had been gone for nearly five years now, and decisions were her responsibility, even when they weighed heavy.

"When did Kevin's father invite you? I didn't know you'd seen them recently." When the Amish school was in session, her boys didn't see much of their Englisch neighbors except on Saturdays.

Timothy shrugged, his wide blue eyes avoiding hers. "I saw Kev when he was waiting for the bus. He said his daad was happy for me to go with them to the spring livestock auction out in Waynesburg."

Timothy was supposed to take his two younger brothers directly to the Amish school by way of the lane. He was usually so reliable, but if he saw Kevin at the bus stop, that meant he'd detoured out to the blacktop road. She filed that away to deal with later.

"I'm sorry, Timothy. I don't think that's a good idea." Waynesburg was a long way off, which meant they'd have to stay overnight.

"Mammi, please. Just because they're Englisch..." Her son let that fade away at her expression, and his face set in a mulish frown. "It's not fair. Daad would have let me."

The words hung there in the air. Dorcas let the reins go slack in her hands. Sadie knew the way to the barn well enough without assistance. Nothing broke the silence but the clack of the mare's shoes and the creak of the wheels. Silas and little Matthew stared, two pairs of blue eyes wide and shocked.

Dorcas had to handle this right, for their sake as well as Timothy's. She took a deep breath, searching for the words.

"Timothy, when Daadi passed, we agreed we'd always try to do what he would want, ain't so? Do you really think he would want this?"

Timothy held the frown for a second longer. Then it washed from his face, and his lips trembled. Tears welled in his eyes. He wiped them away with his hand, sniffing.

"N-no," he mumbled, head down. He hesitated another moment and then slid across the seat to press against her. "I'm sorry, Mammi."

Relief swept through her. She put her arm around him, and his head was hard against her shoulder. Timothy was so aware of being the oldest that he didn't often seek a hug, and she treasured the momentary embrace.

"Yah. I know." She patted him. "It's all right." She murmured a silent prayer of thanks as Sadie stopped at the hitching post. "Komm, now, let's take care of Sadie and then take your school things inside, yah?"

Everyone seemed only too happy to

leave the difficult moments behind. The three boys jumped down and began taking the harness off. Matty, who at six hated to admit to being the smallest, was determined to help. At a glance from her, Timothy lifted him so that he could unfasten the headstall. Matty beamed as it came free.

"I did it. See, Mammi, I did it!"

"You surely did." She smiled, her glance meeting Timothy's. Each time she saw the older ones helping Matty, she seemed to recall Luke showing them their baby brother, telling them that they were the big brothers now.

Timothy turned Sadie out into the paddock and then came back to the barn to help hang up the harness. Watching him, Dorcas thought again about the livestock auction. She'd heard good things about the Waynesburg auction, and given Timothy's interest, she'd have been happy to say yes to any of their relatives. But she'd seen Jeff Brownlee with his own son, and she hadn't been impressed. He yelled at his boy a lot, but as far as she could tell, he never followed through with anything.

Was she being overprotective? Perhaps, but…

Matty came racing out of the barn and grabbed her hand, tugging her toward the door. "Mammi, komm. Schnell! It's Goldilocks. It is. She's sleeping. Shh."

Goldilocks? She remembered how he'd giggled at the picture of three bears standing around the girl in the tiny bed. But what did he imagine he'd seen in the barn?

She stepped inside, pausing for a moment to let her eyes get accustomed to the dim light. What…?

Timothy and Silas were standing in the loose straw in the nearest stall. Shushing her again, Matty led her to them, tiptoeing. "See?" he whispered.

A girl was curled up in the straw. Her kapp had tumbled off, and her corn-colored hair had loosened from its bun. Goldilocks, indeed. Dorcas had to smile, even though she was instantly concerned.

The girl was Amish, clearly. But Dorcas knew every young girl in the church district, and she'd never seen this one before. Had she? Something seemed slightly familiar, but she couldn't put a name to her.

As if feeling their eyes upon her, the girl's lashes fluttered. She stretched, reaching up as her eyes opened… Blue eyes, just as bright a blue as her boys' eyes were. For a moment she just looked at them, and then she scrambled to her feet, a smile lighting her face.

"I'm here. I made it. Are you surprised

to see me? Cousin Dorcas, don't you know me?"

The question was directed at Dorcas, and for another moment her mind was blank. "I…don't… It's not Katie? Katie Unger?"

And then the girl's arms were wrapped around her in a hug. "I've changed, ain't so?"

Dorcas, her mind swirling, hugged her back. "Katie! I haven't seen you since…" She hesitated.

"Since Mammi died," Katie finished for her. "I've grown up some since then."

"You certain sure have." Holding Katie's hand, she turned to the boys, who were looking on, their eyes bright with interest and curiosity. "Boys, this is your cousin, Katie Unger. Her mamm was like a big sister to me when I was a little girl. Katie, here is Timothy, and Silas, and Matthew."

Katie's smile seemed to envelop all of them. "My mamm told me about your family. She always said you were her little sister." Her face clouded. "That's why I came to you, Cousin Dorcas. Please, you have to help me."

The girl's voice had grown passionate with those last words, and she squeezed Dorcas's hand tightly. "Please, please help me."

"Yah, of course." There was no question about that. But what on earth had brought the girl here? How did she even get here? So many questions had to be answered before she could begin to understand what was happening.

Still, first things first. She patted Katie's shoulder, thinking of Mary Ann patting hers when she needed reassurance.

"Komm, let's go inside and get you

something to eat and drink. You must be hungry. And tired."

While ushering all of them toward the door, Dorcas tried to push her thoughts into order. Mary Ann had passed away when Katie was only ten or so.

When Katie's father passed in an accident, his older brother Jacob Unger had taken on responsibility for the child. What was Katie doing here? Surely she hadn't come all the way from Ohio alone.

"Yah, let's go in. But I don't need to eat. I need to tell you." Still holding Dorcas's hand, Katie peered out of the barn as if looking for something. Then she hurried her toward the house, rushing her along.

Just as they reached the back porch, Silas, who was trailing behind, called out, "Mammi, there's a car pulling in the lane. I don't know who it is."

Katie gasped, her rosy cheeks going white. “It’s Onkel Jacob. Hide me. Please, please hide me. If he sees me, he’ll take me back.” She bolted into the house, the boys with her, and all Dorcas could do was follow, her mind fumbling for answers.

She closed the door and tried to speak calmly. “Now, Katie, you have to sit down and tell me quietly what is wrong. How can I help you if you don’t?”

“No, no.” Katie was practically dancing with impatience. She turned to the boys. “Hide me, quick. It’s him.”

The boys apparently had no doubts. Grasping her hands, they rushed her up the stairs, with Matty pushing her from behind.

“Tell him I’m not here.” Katie threw the words over her shoulder, frantic.

As Dorcas tried to call them back, a car pulled up by the back porch. Even from here she could see that in addition to the Englisch driver, there was an Amish passenger. He got out, stretching. Big, broad, with a reddish-brown beard and a stern, determined face.

Jacob Unger. She'd seen him a few times over the years. He wasn't a man who'd believe a lie, even if she were willing to tell him one, which she wasn't. Dorcas took a deep breath, pressed her hands against her skirt to steady them and walked firmly toward the back door, murmuring a quick prayer for guidance.

Jacob glanced back at the driver who'd brought him this far, complaining most of the way. "This won't take long."

"Better not," the man grumbled, leaning on the steering wheel. "I told you before, I have to be back by six, no later. You're not ready in half an hour, I'm going."

Finding a driver to take him in search of his runaway niece had been difficult, but he certain sure wouldn't be calling on this one again. At least he'd finally reached Lost Creek. For sure Katie would be here. Her friend Julie had been only too ready to spill the information once she was confronted.

And what his cousin Ada had been thinking to encourage that friendship, he couldn't imagine. Katie was flighty enough without getting ideas from an Englisch teenager.

A quick glance at the frame house showed no signs of life. Usually someone would look out a window when a car drove in. He strode up to the back porch firmly. The driver was no more eager to get home than he was. His business, making specialty metal parts for an Englisch company, needed his attention, to say nothing of his plans for expansion. This had been a bad time for Katie to act up.

Annoyance lent extra power to his knock on the back door. He caught a flicker of movement at the window, but no sound of footsteps approaching, so he knocked again. If Dorcas Bitler thought she was going to take Katie's side, she'd have another think coming.

He raised his fist for another knock, and the door opened, leaving him with his fist raised in the woman's face. Dorcas Bitler, naturally. He'd last seen her at Mary Ann's funeral, and she hadn't changed much—the same smooth, oval face and clear green eyes, but she wasn't wearing her usual warm smile. He drew his hand back, telling himself he wasn't embarrassed.

"I've come to pick up Katie. Send her out. Please," he added.

Dorcas seemed to stiffen just a little.

"Jacob. How nice to see you after all this time. How are you?"

The determined politeness was an obvious rebuke to his sharpness, and he clenched his jaw.

"I'll be better once I've picked up my niece and headed for home. I assume she's here." He didn't doubt it, or Dorcas wouldn't be acting this way. "I don't have time to waste." He looked over her shoulder, but the kitchen was empty.

"Please, come in." She stepped back from the door. "Would you like some coffee? Or a glass of lemonade?"

"Nothing. Denke." He moved inside, taking another look. There was no sign anyone else was there. "I don't mean to rush you, but Katie is my responsibility." He had a quick flash of concern. "She is here, isn't she?"

Dorcas's expression eased a little, as if his concern pleased her. Well, she should know he was worried. Katie was his niece, after all.

"Sure you won't have some coffee?" She gestured toward the pot on the stove. "It won't take a minute."

"That's very kind of you, Dorcas, but delaying won't help anything. The sooner Katie and I are on our way home, the better. She's started enough talk already."

Dorcas didn't look impressed. If anything, she seemed a little amused. "I take it Katie is quite a handful, just like her mother was. Come, let's have a talk about the problem."

"I don't have time." Didn't the woman understand that she had nothing to say in the matter? A sound from beyond the kitchen caught his ear. "Is Katie upstairs?"

He took two steps toward the hall that must lead to the stairway. Before he could go any farther, the door was blocked. Three boys stood there like identical stair steps, all blond and blue-eyed.

Fuming, he looked from them to Dorcas. Her boys, obviously. "You can't keep me away from my own niece."

He'd meant that to sound authoritative. People usually listened to that tone. But Dorcas's lips quirked.

"Komm now, Jacob. You can't really storm upstairs to my bedrooms without my permission, now can you?"

If he spent much more time with this woman, his jaw would tighten into this permanently locked position. What was worse, he had a feeling she was laughing at him. And even worse, that she was right.

He fought with himself for another moment. Then he shrugged heavily. "If you must, go ahead and talk."

Dorcas's face relaxed into the smile he remembered, and her clear green eyes seemed to lighten. "Gut." She picked up the coffeepot again, giving him a questioning look. "Some coffee with the conversation?"

He jerked an impatient nod, yanking out one of the chairs at the kitchen table. Just as he sat down, a scraping noise sounded just above them. It halted him halfway down.

"That sounds like a window." He glanced toward the ceiling. "If she's trying to get out, it won't help."

"Then I guess we'd best go and see, ain't so?" Touching his sleeve, Dorcas led him toward the door. A glance at her sons collected them. "You, too."

Once out the back door, they walked a few feet out into the yard, past a row of bright yellow daffodils and purple hyacinths, before they had a view of the porch roof. Sure enough, Katie was balancing there, looking as if she didn't know whether to go forward or back.

"Katie." Jacob forced himself to remain outwardly calm. "Come down at once. Haven't you caused enough trouble? It's time to go home."

Her response was predictable, her pert, lively face screwing into a frown. "I won't. You can't make me."

The car horn blared, shouting the driver's impatience, and whatever calmness Jacob had had disappeared.

"You'll do as I say. I'm your uncle, and I'm responsible for you. Come down."

"I won't!" She backed away from the edge as if looking for another escape. "I won't, I won't!"

"Katie Unger, get down here this minute!" To his dismay he found he was shouting back. He never shouted. He never needed to. There was nothing in his well-ordered life to cause it.

Katie opened her mouth, probably to shout something else, but Dorcas spoke, her voice cutting cool and crisp between them. "Enough of that, both of you. Katie, stop being so foolish. Are you planning to spend your life on the roof?"

He was about to agree with her, but then her gaze cut toward him. "And you, Jacob, should act your age. You know perfectly well that even if you can take her back, you can't keep her there."

Jacob stared at her, feeling as if his mouth was hanging open. Then, unable to resist, he chuckled, and he saw her quick smile in response.

After a quick struggle with himself, he nodded. "Yah, all right. I admit it. We're both being foolish." He looked up at his stubborn niece. "Come down, please, Katie. Let's talk about this, yah?"

The stubborn expression faded. She came to the edge of the roof and looked down. And took an abrupt step back, wobbling a bit. "I… I can't."

Dorcas let out a sigh and turned to her sons. "Go up and get her."

They headed for the nearest porch post, and she sighed again, shaking her head. "Not that way. Go up the stairs and help her back in through the window."

The two older ones hopped down at once. The little one hung on a moment longer before he, too, dropped down and charged after his brothers.

Jacob's gaze met hers, and his lips twitched. "Now the coffee?"

Dorcas's laugh seemed to bubble out of her. "I guess so."

They walked together toward the back door. Well, he'd get back later than he'd intended. He could make some phone calls, be sure everything was going all right.

They rounded the house. The first thing he saw was his duffel bag, sitting at the side of the lane. The second was the car and driver disappearing down the road.

Temper flared. He took a few long strides after the car and realized how futile it was. He turned to Dorcas, ready to blame her, but realized in time how foolish that would sound.

A smile tugged at her mouth, but she didn't let it loose. "Your driver seems to be impatient."

Just like you. The words seemed to hang in the air.

He would not get into a shouting match with her the way he had with Katie.

"Yah." He picked up the bag. They proceeded toward the kitchen where he could hear the boys and Katie, apparently helping themselves to something to eat.

He glanced at Dorcas's unruffled face. "I hope you have some idea what I'm going to do with Katie now that I'm stuck here."

"It will work out," she said serenely. "No need to worry."

He closed his lips on all the things he was tempted to say and followed her into the house.

One step forward, Dorcas thought. At least she'd gotten them to stop shouting at each other. That might give her a respite to think of something that could help. So far she'd just been trying to stay calm in the midst of the storm between two obviously self-willed people.

She ushered them all to a seat at the table, amused to see that Matthew had grabbed a chair next to his Goldilocks.

Her sweet Matty had an open heart as well as a talent for wandering into mischief, but he was always well-intentioned. Just now he was pushing the plate of snickerdoodles toward his new cousin, ignoring the fact that Silas was reaching for it.

Katie was smiling, the dimples in her cheeks so like Mary Ann's that it gave Dorcas's heart a little jolt to see them. All the upheaval hadn't affected the girl's appetite—she downed three cookies before Timothy had gotten through one, and he was usually her big eater. Pleasant, smiling, chattering to the boys…and pointedly ignoring her uncle.

Jacob was scowling again, looking at the piece of shoofly pie she offered him as if it might be poison. Neither of them were behaving very well, but he was certain sure old enough to know better, to say nothing of being old enough to put on a pleasant front.

He just might be out of practice at that. From what she remembered of Mary Ann's few letters, he ran his business and his life as if he expected everyone to fall in line, and for the most part, they did.

Get them talking, she told herself. But how?

"Are the Amish schools still open out where you are?" she asked. "Ours will go until the end of May, though the Englisch schools run longer."

Nobody said anything. She wasn't sure that Jacob had even heard her, his mind seemed so far away.

"I like getting out in May," Timothy said, and she gave him a look of thanks. "I'd hate to ride that noisy school bus that Kev takes."

"Not me. That would be fun." Matty produced a zooming sound, mimicking a driver steering.

"You'd be scared," Silas retorted. "Wouldn't he, Timothy?" Silas, always in the middle, bounced back and forth between siding with one brother and then the other.

"Would not," Matty said, but he didn't sound as if he wanted to get into one of their endless rounds of yes you would, no you wouldn't.

Maybe he hadn't liked hearing it between Katie and Jacob. She couldn't help glancing at Jacob. She found him looking at her as if he'd been thinking exactly that, and she flushed.

Don't be ferhoodled, she told herself. He couldn't know. He was too busy trying to decide how he'd get his own way.

Jacob seemed to make an effort at a pleasant expression. "Katie..." he began.

"I'm not going back to Cousin Ada," she said quickly.

"There's nothing wrong with Ada. She's a good woman." His tone was controlled, maybe a little defensive. But his brown eyes had darkened until they were almost black, probably a sign of temper.

"How would you know? You're never around." Katie's voice started to go up, and just like that, Dorcas saw the situation going out of her control.

Before she could say anything, she heard a buggy in the lane. Matty hopped off his chair and headed for the window.

"It's Onkel James and Aunt Sarry." He bolted for the door, and Dorcas felt like racing him out...anything to interrupt the tension.

"My brother and sister," she explained to Jacob. "We'll have to help bring the grocery order in."

She glanced at the boys, but they were already on their way, taking Katie with them.

"I thought you were going to help me talk to Katie..." he began, but she gestured toward the door before he could go any further.

"Come out and meet them," she said. Without waiting, she hustled out, trusting an inspiration was going to strike.

They looked like a swarm of bumblebees around the buggy, which was always the impression when her lively family gathered in one place. Her brother James snatched Matty from a standing position on the buggy seat, tucking him under his arm like a parcel. Sarry, her younger sister, climbed down and then trotted to Dorcas to envelop her in a hug.

"Home," she announced, grinning. Then she spotted Jacob and headed for him.

Dorcas usually judged people by their first reaction to her sister, who had Down syndrome. Sarry loved everyone, and she didn't hesitate to show it. Dorcas didn't have much hope of a good response from Jacob Unger, but to her surprise, he didn't bat an eye when Sarry hugged him.

"I'm Sarry. Short for Sarah," she said as always.

"I'm Jacob." He gave her a real smile, not just a polite one.

Taken aback by the genuineness of that smile, Dorcas blinked. If Jacob could be persuaded to show that side of himself to Katie and maybe even to her, this situation might not be as challenging as she'd thought. But that would make him a very different man than she thought he was.

Still, her task was clear. Whatever it took, here was the one last thing she could do for her dear cousin. It wouldn't be easy, but somehow she had to make peace between Katie and her Onkel Jacob.

Now Jacob's smile was gone, and once

again he was frowning at her. No, it wouldn't be easy at all. In fact, it might be impossible.

Chapter Two

While everyone helped with the unloading, Dorcas found she was wishing for a few more hours in the day…or at least to get rid of Jacob Unger for some part of it. He clearly wanted to get the situation settled with Katie, but Dorcas hadn't had even a minute to talk with the girl alone. Surely he could understand that, couldn't he?

Given the impatient glances Jacob kept sending her way, she couldn't quite convince herself of that. Her brother came into the house, helping Silas carry a ten-pound bag of flour that left a dusting across the kitchen floor.

"In the bin in the pantry," she directed them, wondering why everything her family did left a trail behind.

Her brother seemed to read her mind. "Here, you show me the flour bin, and Silas will get the broom and dustpan to clean up, ain't so, Silas?"

Silas, always eager to impress his uncle, nodded briskly, letting his end of the bag droop to deposit another dusting. James grinned at her as she snatched the bag and together they dumped it into the bin. "Got yourself into another pickle, I see," he commented.

"What's a little spilled flour?" She hoped that was what he meant, but she didn't think so.

"You know what I mean. What's going on with Katie? The boys said she ran away from her uncle." His cheerful, freckled face couldn't look solemn if he tried, and his lips quirked. The two of them had looked enough alike as children that folks had thought they were twins, but she was afraid she might have lost some of that good cheer.

With a quick glance to be sure neither Katie nor Jacob was within earshot, Dorcas blew out an exasperated breath. "That's about the size of it. But her uncle was hot on her heels. She's looking to me for help, and Jacob Unger is probably wishing I'd never been born. And I don't even know what it's all about."

James chuckled. "Can't be that bad. You're gut at talking sense into people. How about a little peacemaking? That's your specialty, ain't so?"

Her brother had always claimed she was the family peacemaker, but right now she doubted it. "I'd like to, if I could only get them to calm down and talk. At the moment, I'd settle for a little time to get Katie's story. If Jacob would clear out for a bit, maybe I could find out what's really wrong."

James dusted flour off his black pants. "If he's spending the night in Lost Creek, he'll have to find a place to sleep. How about if I remove him for that?"

She eyed him skeptically. "Seriously? You think you can?"

"You should know your bruder better than to ask that," he said, laughing. "Just watch me."

Dorcas patted his cheek. "I'll make you an apple crumb pie if you get him out of here for a couple of hours."

"I'll do anything for your apple crumb pie, especially since Mammi is off to Lancaster County where she's probably making one for our brother-in-law right now. Watch and learn."

"And I suppose Grossmammi hasn't

been giving you anything to eat while Mammi and Daad are away," she said, laughing. Their parents had departed yesterday to help her sister Grace, who was soon to have a baby. "Let's see you in action, and then you'll get the pie."

Dorcas drifted along behind her younger brother as he headed outside. Not surprisingly, Katie and Jacob had taken advantage of her absence to start arguing again. When Dorcas stepped outside, she heard Katie repeating what she herself had said, that he could take Katie home but he couldn't make her stay there.

Dorcas gave James a little push. "Go on, before they get any more wound up."

Smiling, James sauntered over to the buggy. "Hey, Jacob, I hear you need a place to stay tonight. Komm along with me. We're just across the road. We'll give you supper, and I'll call to get you a room at the Amish Inn."

"Denke, but I need to talk to your sister." Jacob glanced at Dorcas, his eyes darkening, and she quickly occupied herself with the last load Timothy was carrying in. But she could still hear their voices.

"You won't get any sense out of Dorcas until after she gets all these kids fed. Supper time here is like feeding time at the zoo. We'll have a peaceful supper, and you can borrow a buggy to drive down to the inn. Okay?"

There was silence for a moment, and she waited, ears pricked.

"Ach, I guess you're right." He didn't sound very sure. "Let me just tell her." After another pause, he seemed to think he'd missed something. "Denke. I appreciate it."

Hearing him approach, she called out to her sister, "Sarry, will you show Katie the room next to yours? She can sleep there."

"I will." Sarry gave Katie her face-splitting smile and put her arm around her waist. "Komm."

Relieved to have one of the combatants out of the way, Dorcas turned to find Jacob right behind her.

"Your bruder says I should go with him now to get set up for tonight. You want to get rid of me, ain't so?"

"No, I..." She felt herself flushing. "Well, I haven't had a chance to talk to Katie yet. I'd like to find out what made her run away, if I can."

Jacob's hand brushed that away impatiently. "You'll find nothing but nonsense, but if you must, then go ahead."

Her eyebrows lifted. "Nonsense? It must be pretty big nonsense to make her run all the way from Bellport to Lost Creek."

"Only in Katie's mind, I'd think."

For an instant she thought he was going to insist on talking now, but he shook his head, turning away. She touched his arm to stop him for a moment.

"If it's just in her mind, then that's all the more reason to find out what it is. Don't you see that?" Her voice was a bit more pleading than she'd intended, and she wished she'd left well enough alone.

But he turned then, touching her hand briefly as he did so. "Yah, I suppose you're right at that." He looked baffled and annoyed at the feeling. "I never claimed to be able to understand teen-age girls."

She almost pointed out that he'd once been a teenager himself but decided to hold her tongue. She took a step back, hoping her smile looked polite. "James will take good care of you. I'll see you after supper… Say about seven?"

For an instant she thought he'd argue about the time, but then he nodded. "Yah, all right. Denke," he added reluctantly and stalked off to the buggy.

Dorcas let out a relieved breath. At last she had some thinking time. Now to tackle Katie. She had to find out what was behind all of this before she could hope to do anything about it.

Dorcas sent the boys off to do their chores. Katie looked as if she'd like to go with them, but Dorcas drew her into the kitchen along with Sarry. This was probably as alone as they'd get.

"We'd best hurry along with supper, or your uncle will be back before we know it. I have some beef stew in the pantry, so I'll heat that up while you and Sarry make biscuits."

Katie blinked. "Make biscuits? But I don't know how."

Dorcas exchanged a startled glance with Sarry. Any Amish girl of fifteen surely ought to know something that simple.

"Just follow along with Sarry. She can show you, ain't so, Sarry?"

"Yah, for sure." Sarry began clattering bowls together, and in a few minutes they were all three working.

Dorcas wasn't sure what to tackle first, but maybe finding out what Katie's life was like with that cousin of Jacob's was a good step. "What is your favorite thing to make, Katie?"

The girl, intent on measuring out flour as Sarry showed her, just shrugged. "I guess I don't really cook anything. Except popcorn. I do make that sometimes."

Sarry stared. "Just popcorn? Nothing else?"

"I'd like to do it, but every time I try,

Cousin Ada just chases me out of the way and says she can do it faster herself."

Now it was Dorcas's turn to look startled. It was inconceivable that the woman was raising the girl without teaching her something so important to life. She insisted that even her boys must learn to make a few simple things.

"What do you do now that you're out of school? Are you working someplace?"

Katie, rolling out the biscuit dough under Sarry's direction, shook her head. "I could have got a job at the Amish Buffet, but Cousin Ada said that Onkel Jacob wouldn't like it." She thumped the rolling pin down on the counter. "Everything I want to do it's the same thing... Onkel Jacob wouldn't like it."

She wasn't sure what to make of the

picture Katie was making of her life. Was she exaggerating? Probably.

"Have you talked to Onkel Jacob about it?"

Katie made a face that was so like her mother at that age that Dorcas felt her heart clench.

"He's always too busy with the factory. Whenever I ask him about anything, he says to do what Cousin Ada says. And Cousin Ada is hopeless. She thinks a girl should just stay home and be good. She even said I don't need to worry about meeting boys, because when I'm old enough, Onkel Jacob will take care of that."

Sarry started to giggle and Dorcas had trouble suppressing a laugh. "It sounds as if Cousin Ada has very old-fashioned ideas. Maybe if I talk to your uncle, we can get him to see that."

"It is old-fashioned, ain't so?" Katie's

face brightened for a moment. "That's what I thought." Her expression drooped. "But it won't do any good. He always says to ask Cousin Ada. Anybody would think that she knew all about life, and she's never even been married!"

Again Dorcas had to suppress a laugh, but it really wasn't funny. On the surface it seemed they just weren't listening to each other, but there had to be more to it than that.

Sarry had started setting the table, and Katie helped her without being asked. She seemed to be willing enough, and Dorcas had another disapproving thought about the unknown Cousin Ada. If a child was willing, you taught, even if it was inconvenient, even if you could do it faster yourself. Every Amish child learned to do things by working alongside someone older. That was a fact of

Amish life that Cousin Ada seemed to have missed.

If she had intervened when the decisions were made about Katie's future, might that have helped? But she'd been a new widow then with three small boys to raise. She couldn't have taken on Katie, too, any more than she could now.

So why did she feel so guilty?

The stew was heated through, just needing to be dipped up, and the biscuits smelled about ready. The boys would be stampeding back in soon. She'd better ask any other questions quickly, starting with the one that her guilt had pushed to the top of her mind.

"Katie, tell me, please. What exactly made you decide to run away? And why did you come here? What did you think I could do?"

Katie stopped with a bunch of silverware in her hand. "Exactly?" She flushed a little. “I guess it will sound silly, but it wasn’t. The parents at church were going to have a singing for the kids who were coming up to rumspringa. All of us. And Cousin Ada said I couldn’t go. She said Onkel Jacob wouldn’t like it. And I tried to ask Onkel Jacob, and he didn’t even listen to me. He just said Cousin Ada knew best. And she didn’t!”

Dorcas had to bite her tongue to keep from agreeing. “Why here? What do you want me to do?”

Katie dropped the silverware with a clatter. “Let me stay here. Please. You will, won’t you? Mammi would want that. Let me live with you.”

There it was…the thing she couldn’t imagine coping with. But she also couldn’t find the words to reject Katie. The boys rushed in, Silas carrying eggs in a basket and Matty with a yellow mum, which he presented to Katie.

Dorcas watched her boys, laughing and chattering with Katie. She was tempted, but hardened her heart. She couldn't take on another child by herself. And even if she could, how would she hold out against Jacob Unger?

If Jacob had been looking for a respite from Dorcas's busy family, he didn't find it at James's house. The only reason he could see for James and Dorcas's obvious desire to send him off here was to get him away from Katie…certainly not for any peace and quiet.

He thought longingly of his small house next to the factory, neat and tidy and above all quiet. James had a wife, Anna, lively and talkative, and three children, ranging from a bubbly four-year-old girl to a two-year-old boy to a baby daughter, and supper with all of them was far noisier than all of the factory machinery running at the same time.

Planting a stiff smile on his face, he ate what was set before him and wished he had a cotton ball to stuff in his right ear next to the crying baby. Neither James nor Anna seemed to notice the noise, talking cheerfully over it.

Was it possible he was getting old and grumpy? Maybe so, but Jacob didn't see how anyone could think with the infant crying, the two-year-old trying to climb out of his high chair and the little girl showing off how she could recite her numbers at the top of her lungs.

To his relief, Anna took the baby off to put him to bed, and James supervised the other two while they carried their plates to the sink. Jacob's ears rang in the sudden quiet.

Jacob looked at James and suspected James was laughing at him.

"It's a bit noisy here at supper time, too. I guess I'm so used to it that it feels normal to me." He pushed his chair back into place at the table. "We can hitch up the buggy when you're ready to go to the inn, but Dorcas's place is just across the road."

"Denke." Jacob glanced at the large round clock over the counter. "I need to make a couple of phone calls first, though…to set up a driver for tomorrow and also to check in with the factory."

"Sure thing." James untangled himself from his small daughter and led the way to the back door. "Phone shanty's outside, and I'll give you a couple of numbers to try for a driver."

They walked outside, and James let the screen door swing to, holding it so his small son couldn't push his way out. "I hear you've got quite a business out in Bellport. Must keep you busy, ain't so?"

He nodded, eager to get to the phone. "I don't like being out of touch. Thanks to Katie, it was..." He hesitated, trying to find a word that didn't express his annoyance with Katie, to say nothing of Dorcas. "...unavoidable."

James grinned. "So I gather. I remember her mother from when we were kids. Mary Ann was pretty lively, too."

"So your sister said."

"Dorcas is good with kids. Give her a little time with Katie. You won't regret it."

So apparently James didn't have any trouble detecting his feelings about Dorcas, but at least he didn't seem to be annoyed in his turn. Were all the Miller family as unruffled as the ones he'd met?

"If your sister can get Katie to listen to sense, I'll be grateful." It sounded stilted, but it was the best he could do. If Katie hadn't thought she'd find shelter with

Dorcas, she might never have tried this foolishness.

"There you are." James pointed to the small white shanty that was attached to the side of a chicken coop. "I've got some names and numbers posted for drivers. I'd start with the top one. Just say you're visiting us."

"Denke. I'll leave some money for the calls."

"Ach, don't be foolish. You're our guest. You'll want to let your assistant know when you'll be getting back, ain't so?"

He nodded, his thoughts bouncing around in his head. What had been going on today? Would Reuben have had any problems? Had he taken care of any new orders? The long list was clear in his mind, but that didn't help Reuben.

"One thing about running a family dairy operation—everybody knows what to do," James pointed out, seeming in no hurry to leave him alone. “Hope you’ve got a good assistant.”

“I run things myself,” he said stiffly. “You’re very like your sister.”

James shrugged. “Ach, no. Not nearly as organized. She often helps a cousin with running a quilt and fabric shop, besides keeping the farm going and looking after Sarry and the kids. Never lets anything trouble her, though.”

He didn’t have an answer to that. James obviously thought highly of his sister. He could hardly argue about it.

Jacob moved toward the shanty, hoping James would take the hint and leave him alone. “Denke,” he said firmly.

Still smiling, James turned back into the kitchen. “I’ll get the mare harnessed up whenever you want it.” He hesitated, looking as if he intended to say something more. To tell him to listen to Dorcas, maybe?

Jacob picked up the receiver. He probably wouldn't have any choice about listening to her, but she wasn't going to change his mind about anything. Phillip had left his daughter to his care, and Jacob had every intention of living up to his obligation no matter what anyone else thought. Especially Dorcas Bitler.

Chapter Three

Dorcas glanced at the kitchen clock. Jacob should be coming back shortly, and she set cups and plates out in case he was willing to relax enough to share coffee and pie.

She'd decided to speak to him first, if he'd agree. The tale of all the restrictions that his cousin had put on Katie might come better from her. Or, at least, more calmly. She couldn't rely on Katie to stay calm.

As for Jacob...well, he was old enough

to know better than to overreact. Or was he?

The kitchen window showed her Jacob approaching the house and set her nerves jangling. Now who was overreacting?

Dorcas continued to watch from the window as Jacob drew near, rounding the hitching rail. She realized that she was trying to read his emotions from his face.

Stepping back from the window, she smoothed her apron down and headed for the door with a silent prayer for wisdom. She would need it.

Dorcas held the door open, and Jacob came in, nodding politely. His face told her exactly nothing. It was back to the firm expression that seemed so natural to him.

"Wilkom, Jacob. Komm." She gestured him to the table.

He glanced around the kitchen, quiet

except for the chatter of the kinder from the living room. The boys had talked Katie and Sarry into playing one of their favorite board games. She had warned them of dire consequences for anyone who came to the kitchen without being called, and she could only hope they'd remember.

Jacob had pulled out the chair she'd indicated, but he had yet to sit down. "I thought this talk was supposed to include Katie."

She set the mugs of coffee on the table and slid into her own chair. At her look, he sat, but there was nothing relaxed or comfortable about it.

"Katie?" he repeated.

"I thought it might be best if we talked together first." She slid the sugar bowl toward him and hoped her fingers weren't shaking. Jacob might make his employees quake in their shoes, but not her. "Is that all right with you?"

The slight smile that touched his firm lips made her wonder if he knew what she was thinking. But he just picked up the mug, holding it between his hands. "Do I have a choice?"

Her own lips twitched. "I hope not. You're not going to want to hear some of the things Katie had to say about your cousin."

"Ada?" His voice lifted, and he really did look startled.

"Yah, Ada. It's the only cousin of yours I know about, ain't so?"

"Anybody more patient and agreeable I've never met. If Katie's complaining about her, it just shows how silly her troubles are."

"Did you ever think that Ada might be different with you than with Katie?"

He frowned slightly. "Well, she has to

exercise some control over Katie. What else would you expect?"

"According to Katie, every time she brings a problem to you, you tell her that she has to do what Cousin Ada says."

"Well, naturally. When I took on the guardianship, I knew I'd have to have help. Cousin Ada seemed a logical choice. I asked her to take over Katie." His muscles tightened as if he was about to get up and walk away. "I don't know anything about teenage girls. That's why I'm paying Ada to look after her."

"So you agree when Ada says she can't stay over at a friend's house, and she can't get a job now that she's out of school, and that she's not supposed to drive the pony cart or talk to boys or even go to the get-together the parents planned for those coming up to rumspringa age?"

"Is that what Katie says?" He sounded

disbelieving. "It's just like I said—exaggerated. Ada wouldn't..."

"Are you sure? Do you know that yourself, or is that just what you want to believe?" She prayed she hadn't gone too far, but he had to be made to listen.

Jacob opened his mouth and then seemed to reconsider what he was going to say. He frowned, staring down at the table. "All right. If it's true, I agree it sounds far too strict. But you only have Katie's word for it."

"She's the one we're concerned about, ain't so? The one your bruder trusted you to take care of."

"And I've tried to live up to my bruder's wishes." He spoke stiffly, but Dorcas could see a flicker of doubt in his dark eyes. Was she finally getting through to him?

"I'm sure you have," she said gently. "But a fifteen-year-old is different from a five-year-old. I'm certain sure she's more difficult than my Matty, for instance."

"I guess." He rubbed his temples as if thinking about this was challenging. "I suppose you think you could do it better."

Was that what was really angering him? The idea that someone else knew more about it that he did?

"At least I remember what it was like to be a teenage girl. That helps."

His eyes hardened again. "In other words, they should have appointed you as her guardian instead of me. If you felt that way, why didn't you say anything at the time? I called you when Mary Ann was dying. You didn't get there until the funeral."

Dorcas felt the blood draining from her face as she thought of that terrible time. She grasped the edge of the table.

"When Mary Ann passed, it was just a few months after my husband did. Matty was just a baby. I was barely able to take care of my own kinder at that point."

Now the blood rushed into Jacob's face. She'd never have imagined seeing him so mortified.

"Dorcas, I'm so sorry." He almost stammered the words. "I didn't… I wasn't thinking." He touched her hand lightly—just a gentle brush that conveyed his grief at causing her pain.

"Yah, all right," she managed to say. "The question is, what are you going to do about Katie? And how can I help her?"

Silence stretched between them. Jacob stared down at her hand, lying next to his on the table. Finally he shook his head.

"I'll have to go back to Bellport and talk to Ada. If what Katie says is true, then she's obviously not the right person to guide a teenage girl."

She bit her lip to keep from saying that he should have realized that before and tried to look approving. At least he was doing it now.

"In the meantime, someone must look after Katie," he went on. He shook his head, looking like a man who was dazed from a fall.

"Can't she stay with you?" It didn't seem that difficult to Dorcas.

He frowned at her, as if she'd given the wrong answer on a test. "And leave her alone all day? Have everyone in Bellport gossiping about her, as well as Ada?"

Dorcas could see an obvious answer, but he wouldn't like it. "She could stay here for a visit. I'd enjoy having her, and what would be more natural than for her to spend time with her mother's best friend?"

She was right. He didn't like it. She could see the word *no* forming on his lips, but it didn't come out. Instead, he let out a long breath.

"I have to get back." He said it as if he was talking to himself. "If I'm not there, everything grinds to a halt."

She was tempted to say that no one was that crucial to a business—or more to the point, no one should be. And that business shouldn't come before his niece. It seemed natural to her, but would it to him?

He cleared his throat. "Would you be kind enough to have Katie here for a visit?"

Her smile broke through. "For sure. We'd love it."

"Denke." He put his hand over hers for a brief moment. "You're a good friend for her, Dorcas."

Was she a friend to him, as well? She

doubted he could see her that way, but at least she'd moved a step forward.

Jacob had plenty of time on the ride home the next day to think. About Katie, about her parents, about the mistakes he'd made. Still, how would he have guessed that Cousin Ada would be so foolish in how to deal with a teenage girl?

He could almost hear Dorcas's response. Why didn't you find out?

"Are you a relative of Mrs. Bitler and the Miller family?"

Apparently the driver didn't plan to go all the way in silence. At least he was friendly—a sharp contrast to his last driver.

"A friend." The words sounded brusque, and he thought he'd best say a bit more. "My niece Katie is a cousin of theirs. She's visiting Dorcas… Mrs. Bitler."

The Englischer nodded. "Fine people. And good neighbors. We live just down the road from them." He hesitated and then added, "I'm Charlie, by the way. Charlie Downs."

"Jacob Unger," he responded. "I'm glad you were free to drive me." *Especially after yesterday's miserable trip.*

"Always glad to help out when I can." His heavily tanned face creased in a smile, making him look younger than his white hair would lead a person to believe. "I enjoy driving, and since I retired, it's nice to earn a little extra money. And to have some reason to get out of the house." His grin reappeared. "My wife says she started saving up a list of projects the day she found out I'd be retiring."

Jacob laughed, and taking that for encouragement, Charlie launched into an account of his family, his neighbors, the surrounding area and the history of Lost Creek. If Jacob had wanted time to think, he wouldn't get it.

Still, the man's chatter made the time pass quickly. They stopped for coffee and a snack and reached Bellport in the early afternoon.

As they pulled up at his small house next to the factory, Jacob switched from thinking about his problems with Katie to wondering how the factory was doing without him.

Paying Charlie and assuring him that he'd call him again, Jacob crossed quickly to his front door. He'd just as soon not see anyone from the business until he'd checked the mail and dropped his bag.

His small house was quiet, and as neat as when he'd left. A kitchen, living room and two small bedrooms occupied by one man didn't have much chance to be anything but neat and quiet. The thought of the house he'd shared with Teresa when they first married slid into his mind. He'd liked the house, with its fruit trees and small garden, but he hadn't been able to stay there after Teresa was gone.

Memories flooded his thoughts, and he pushed them out. He didn't want to think about it, and he certain sure didn't have time now. He hurried out the kitchen door, crossed the alley and went into the machine shop through its side door. It couldn't be more convenient, he told himself, filling his mind with business to block out everything else.

It was quieter than he expected. Normally the place was filled with the sounds of people at work. Here was the shop that produced the buckles for the intricate sets of harnesses that made work easier for those who farmed with horses. Or oxen, though there were few of those left. Only two people were at work. They nodded in greeting and went on with what they were doing.

"Where is everyone?" He tried to control his voice, not to blame those who were here and working.

The youngest of the three Fisher brothers looked up, obviously reluctant to speak. Given the way Jacob was staring at him, he found his voice.

"Reuben…he sent some folks home early. A shipment didn't come in, so there was nothing for them to be getting on with."

He glanced at the part he was working on with obvious desire to get back to it. The boy was as gifted with his hands as his brothers, and in addition he had a bright, creative mind. He'd come up with several new ways of updating the traditional parts.

"Denke, Joshua." No point in making the boy uncomfortable with questions he couldn't answer. "I'll check with Reuben."

He strode on through to the center of the building. Here were the computers that carried the precise plans for the variety of parts they made for Englisch businesses. Reuben, who'd been with him since the beginning, would talk for hours about what the computers did for them. It was a good thing, given how hard Jacob had worked to get the bishop to approve their use.

Not seeing Reuben there, he headed for the office. Reuben was on the phone, speaking unusually sharply to someone.

"You know how we feel about late deliveries. If it's not here by noon tomorrow, we'll expect to hear a better explanation if you want to keep our business."

He hung up, and a smile eased his grim expression as he turned to Jacob.

"I'm wonderful glad you're back. Did you get everything settled for Katie?"

"For the moment, I guess." He wasn't eager to share his problems, although he knew he could trust Reuben with anything. "What's going on here?"

As if hearing an unspoken criticism, Reuben slid from the chair behind the desk. He gestured toward the phone.

"That shipment from Dawson's didn't come in. We needed it to get today's work finished." He shrugged. "I finally sent some of the men home. No point in keeping them here with nothing to do."

"You could have started them on something else." Frustrated, Jacob tossed his straw hat on a peg.

Reuben's eyebrows lifted, his blue eyes turning cool. "I didn't know what you wanted to move to next. I tried to call this morning as soon as I knew, but you had already left. I couldn't go scrambling through your papers, now could I?"

The tart words reminded him of the one occasion when Reuben had looked on his desk for some information he needed. His jaw set. He'd probably reacted too sharply, he guessed, but that was no reason…

Well, maybe it was. He felt sure that Dorcas would have thought that. There she was in his mind again. He had to deal with her over Katie, but he certain sure didn't want her involved in his business.

He opened his mouth and then shut it again. He remembered her comment about everyone needing help. He didn't want to, but there it was. Maybe she had a point, but he certain sure wasn't going to admit it.

He pulled the calendar from the wall

and put it on his desk. "I'd best get some goals set out for the next few days."

Nodding, Reuben turned to go.

"Wait." He spoke abruptly, surprised at himself. "Maybe you'd better stay and help me with this. So we'll both know what's going on. And what to do about Dawson's. You're right there. We can't put up with that kind of behavior."

Without a word, Reuben pulled a chair up to the desk, and they got to work.

Dorcas found the next few days happy and trouble free. She'd half expected to find Katie wanting to go here, there and everywhere after the restricted life she'd been leading. But she'd seemed content with the usual family life, playing with the boys, helping with chores, getting Sarry to teach her some simple cookery and most of all chattering away so fast it sometimes made Dorcas dizzy.

At least she'd meet some new people to chatter to at worship this morning. Dorcas chased the last of her family into the buggy and nodded for Timothy to take the lines. Sitting up very straight, Timothy clicked to Sadie, and they moved out the lane to join the line of slowly moving buggies heading for the King farm, where worship would be held this warm spring morning.

Katie leaned forward from the back seat to watch. "Timothy, you're really a good driver. I wish I could drive."

"You can't drive?" Sarry twisted to look at her. "Everybody can drive."

"Even me," Matty popped up.

"You can't." Silas was quick to refute that, and he turned to Katie. "Not really," he confided over Matty insisting he could. "Just the pony cart."

"Well, that's better than I can. Ada always said my onkel would teach me, but he never had time." She didn't sound angry any longer, just resigned.

"Don't feel bad." Sarry emphasized the words with a hug. "We teach you."

Katie's surprise and pleasure lit up her face, and she squeezed Sarry back. "Denke." She wiped away a happy tear.

Dorcas blinked back a happy tear of her own. The relationship between Katie and Sarry was a precious thing, even after such a short time. Katie was like her mother in that way, and it touched Dorcas's heart.

Mary Ann had possessed the same beautiful gift of reacting to every person as he or she was, not younger or older or different. Cranky or sweet, Mary Ann had passed her love along to them, and she seemed to have given that beautiful gift to her daughter. Dorcas turned, clasping Katie's hand in a warm grip.

The King farm wasn't far, and soon

they'd hopped down, turning the buggy over to the King boys, who were acting as hostlers today and seemed very impressed with themselves.

Katie, holding on to Dorcas's arm, was wide-eyed. "Do people here remember my mammi?" she whispered.

"For sure." Dorcas found her throat getting tight. She should have realized Katie might want to hear memories of her mother. "You'll have a chance to talk to them after worship."

The boys rushed off to get in line with their uncle supervising, while James's wife and their little ones joined Dorcas, Sarry and Katie. Katie gave one wistful look at where the girls in her age group were lining up, and then she held out her arms to take Anna's baby daughter.

Dorcas longed for this morning to go well for Katie, and most of all that there was no gossip going around to make her uncomfortable. As far as she could tell, no one seemed to know that her guest was a runaway, and she yearned to keep it that way, for Katie's sake and for her own.

She tried to tell herself that no one could know, but a lifetime of experience in how gossip flew in the Amish community made her uncertain. *Please*, she murmured silently.

The morning service went on its way. Three hours later, when it came to the last prayer, Anna's little ones were asleep. Even while helping with them, Dorcas looked around, trying to find some of the folks who would remember Mary Ann. That would make Katie feel welcome.

But before she could, she saw her aunt Lizzie coming toward her. Her heart sank. There was no chance to get away. Aunt Lizzie's skinny hand gripped her arm like a claw, and her pointed face wore a mixture of curiosity and suspicion.

"Well, Dorcas? Why did I not know about your visitor? You should have told me you were expecting her. I'd have come right over to welcome her."

And that's just why I didn't. She hoped Aunt Lizzie couldn't follow her thoughts.

She touched Katie's arm lightly. "Aunt Lizzie, this is Katie. Cousin Mary Ann's daughter. Katie, my great-aunt."

Lizzie's sharp-featured face drew closer with curiosity. "So you're Mary Ann's child, come to visit at last. Mary Ann never did. Folks don't like that, you know, when someone moves away and forgets us."

Persistence, curiosity, blaming... Lizzie managed to get all of that into a few sentences. Well-meaning, but she was the most tactless person imaginable.

Maybe that was why Aunt Lizzie spent her life rotating from one relative to another. There was no one who could be more help in case of sickness or trouble, but sooner or later, a sharp word or a foolish criticism would lead to a quarrel that sent her on to the next.

"I'm sure Katie doesn't know anything about that," she said firmly. Before Lizzie could charge on with another question, she tried to divert her. "I think Cousin George has been looking for you. Did you talk to him yet?"

"George? What does he want with me? If he's trying to get me to watch those kinder of his while his wife goes gallivanting..."

"Maybe you'd better find out," she suggested. "He might need to know."

Lizzie bridled, releasing her grip on Katie's arm. "I suppose so. But I can tell you—" Suddenly seeing George, she darted off like a hornet buzzing in on a new target.

Dorcas's lips twitched at the sight of Katie's face. "Don't be troubled by Aunt Lizzie. She's a good soul, but she's got more than her share of curiosity, plus a sharp tongue. I'll keep you sheltered."

Katie giggled. "I hope so." She glanced around. "What happened to Sarry?"

"I'm not sure." Dorcas glanced around. "But she'll find us. Komm. I want to make you known to some of the young folk."

It was easier than she expected to make Katie happy. Sarry reappeared, and it turned out she'd rounded up several of the girls who were about Katie's age.

Seeing Katie safely occupied, Dorcas moved away to check on the boys. The two bigger ones were involved in a kick-ball game, while Matty was leaning on

Onkel James's shoulder, whispering in his ear.

The sight pierced her heart, but it also warmed it. She didn't suppose she'd ever stop regretting that Matty didn't know his daadi, but James did his best to fill in the empty spaces for the boys. And his best was very good.

Sally King caught up with her before she could wander any farther. "Ach, it's gut to catch you alone. So that's Mary Ann's girl… We'd know her anyplace, ain't so?"

She nodded, smiling at Sally, who'd been a neighbor of Mary Ann. "You see the resemblance, too, yah? And once in a while she'll say something or move in a way that is just like her mammi. It's like having our Mary Ann back again."

"How did you get that uncle of hers to let her have a visit with you? From everything I've heard, he's not very accommodating."

"How did you get to know that about Jacob Unger? I didn't realize you knew anyone in Bellport."

Sally laughed. "I notice you don't argue about his personality."

"I can't. He's very intent on his own way. But Katie is just as stubborn as he is." She certainly couldn't lie to one of her closest friends about how Katie appeared in their lives, but she wouldn't have to. "With Katie arguing and me pacifying, he decided to let her stay for a bit. But you didn't answer my question. How do you know about him?"

If Sally had too many connections in Bellport, it might be a problem.

"Ach, I don't know all that much," Sally said, to her relief. "My cousin Joseph has dealt with him in the way of business. His machine shop or factory or whatever he calls it does some very specialized parts that Joseph needs in his repair shop."

"Bellport is pretty far away to be dealing with, isn't it?"

Sally shrugged. "I guess they send things back and forth. And Joseph says there's talk that Jacob is looking for a place to open another facility. Maybe he's thinking about coming over this way. Joseph would be pleased."

"Maybe so. He didn't mention anything about it to me." She wasn't sure she liked the possibility, even though it might make it easier to see Katie.

Sally nudged her. "Ask him when you talk to him. Joseph would thank you."

She laughed, picturing herself questioning Jacob about his business. "I don't think Jacob would appreciate my questions about his business. I only know him because of his niece."

"Speaking of Katie, here she is now." Sally nodded toward the approaching teens. "And she's picked up some friends."

Katie was approaching, with Sally King's twin girls as well as three teen boys who seemed to be admiring the girls. Or teasing them. It was sometimes hard to tell at that age.

Katie burst into speech as soon as she was close enough. "Dorcas, guess what? The King family is having a picnic and singing on Thursday night, and they invited me!" Her voice soared at the last word. "Please, please, can I come?"

The other teens were adding their voices to the plea, and Dorcas felt as if she'd fallen smack into a trap. Wasn't that the sort of event that had led to Katie running away? What would Jacob think if she allowed Katie to do the very thing he'd forbidden?

But looking at the pleading faces, she felt as if the decision was already made. Whatever Jacob thought, she was going to say yes.

Chapter Four

Wednesday was a good day for Katie to spend with Sally King's fifteen-year-old twins. The three girls had gotten into the best friends stage very quickly, and she and Sally arranged that Dorcas would stop by to visit in the afternoon and take her home.

As Dorcas's buggy went past the kitchen window, Sally looked out and waved before coming to the door to greet her with a warm hug.

"Come in, come in. I've got the kettle

on, and the girls are upstairs, probably telling each other secrets."

"If I remember that age, they never come to the end of those." Dorcas smiled, seeing the table spread with cookies and streusel coffee cake. "You must think I came hungry."

"The kinder will eat anything we leave, I promise. Any word from your mother yet about your sister's baby? If it should be twins, they usually come early, so know."

"So I've heard," Dorcas said. "You should know, if anyone does. They promised to call, but nothing yet."

"Your parents will probably be there all the longer, anyway. You know what it's like with a first baby. So how are you doing with mothering a teenage girl? Any complaints from Onkel Jacob?" Sally busied herself with the teapot.

"It's not easy," Dorcas admitted. "The

mothering part, I mean. Girls are certain sure different from boys."

Sally chuckled. "They are that. When my boys came along I was amazed at how much easier they seemed to be. But what about Jacob?"

"Actually, I'm surprised that he hasn't been calling every day to check on us. I hope that means he trusts me with Katie." She held out her cup, and Sally poured from the teapot, the stream of tea amber in the light.

The kitchen was on the southwest corner of the house, giving it the afternoon sunshine. It made the cupboard doors gleam and picked up the grain of the wide floorboards. The windowsills were lined with herbs, green and lush already even though it was only April. Dorcas could smell the mint from where she sat.

"Hard to tell what the man is really

like." Sally sliced another wedge of coffee cake. "I asked Cousin Joseph, but he didn't seem to know anything but what I told you already. Joseph thought he'd been a widower for a long time, since there's been no mention of his wife."

Dorcas thought about Katie's words. "According to Katie, he adored his wife so much that he's never looked at another woman since."

Sally eyed her, a smile touching her lips. "Yah, I've heard that expression often enough. It just means he hasn't met the right person to fill the hole in his heart."

"You don't think it's possible for someone to stay faithful, even when the loved one dies?"

Sally frowned in concentration. "Possible? Well, maybe. But awfully lonely for a childless man like Jacob." The frown vanished, and her eyes twinkled. "Are you interested?"

"No," she said quickly. Too quickly, probably, because Sally gave her a knowing look, and Dorcas could feel a flush rising in her face. "Really, Sally. I'm not looking for love again."

"That doesn't mean love isn't looking for you," Sally replied. "All right, I won't tease you. Just don't close any doors, yah?"

"We'll see," she said, the familiar words a mother used when she didn't want to commit to anything.

"Okay, okay. To change the subject, how about coming with Katie to help chaperone the singing tomorrow night? With all those youngers here, we could use another pair of eyes. And it might help you remember more about teenage girls."

"I'm not sure I want to remember that

much," she said, draining her cup. "But I'm glad to help. That way when Jacob Unger complains, I can tell him I was there the whole time."

Dorcas glanced at the clock and rose from her chair. "I'd best get moving. Aunt Lizzie invited herself for supper tonight."

Katie and the twins came down the steps in time to hear the words, and Katie frowned. "I only saw her once, but I don't think Aunt Lizzie likes me."

The twins exchanged glances, and then Betsy blurted out her thought. "We don't think she likes anyone, do we, Becky?"

"Girls, don't talk like that," Sally said briskly.

"Just remember," Dorcas added. "God sends difficult people into our lives so we'll learn patience."

"And I'm still working on that," Sally said, smiling.

Dorcas nodded. When it came to Aunt Lizzie, she definitely was still struggling.

Supper with Aunt Lizzie was a challenge, as it always was. Her sharp eyes flickered around the table as if looking for something wrong. The boys, unusually alert, had their best table manners on display. Katie was sitting between the two younger ones, and she unobtrusively caught a spoon that slid out from under Matty's hand, headed for the floor.

Dorcas tried to keep Aunt Lizzie's conversation on the cousins she'd been staying with, and the flow gushed out like water into the bathtub. Aunt Lizzie always had something to say, and in this case, it was mostly favorable. Dorcas began to relax. She'd been afraid this supper might have been aimed at a request to come and stay for a time.

Sarry sat with her gaze fixed on her plate. Maybe she didn't want to draw Aunt Lizzie's attention. It seemed, now that Dorcas thought about it, that Sarry had been awfully quiet from the time she and Katie had returned.

Dorcas watched her for a moment, concerned, but then Aunt Lizzie demanded a response, and she pulled her attention back. It was best that she tried to keep Lizzie occupied… It was certain sure that the kinder didn't want to answer any of her questions. They'd either come up with the wrong answer or they'd lose the power of speech entirely. Luke had once said Lizzie had the same effect on him.

A smile tilted her lips as she remembered that evening. Luke had also wanted to know why they had a prickly pear in their family garden. She'd said everyone had at least one, but Luke denied that his family did.

Every family had at least one difficult member, she told herself. But she was still happy when supper was over and the table cleared.

Katie and the boys scattered as quickly as possible in search of chores that would take them outside. Dorcas wasn't surprised, and she glanced at Sarry to exchange a smile, but didn't get a response.

Aunt Lizzie, she was happy to see, was pulling on her sweater in preparation for leaving. She was looking out the back door, watching the kinder, but she turned back suddenly to catch Dorcas's eye.

"Why did you let that girl rush out instead of helping with the dishes? It's the least she could do, coming here so unexpectedly."

As it happened, she had a ready answer for that. "Sarry and I like doing the dishes together. It's a nice time to chat, just the two of us. Ain't so, Sarry?"

Sarry nodded enthusiastically. She was probably just as eager as the boys were to see Aunt Lizzie drive off.

Her great-aunt wasn't finished with her thoughts on Katie, though. "How does she have time to come here? Doesn't she have a job? That uncle of hers ought to realize that it's imposing on you, handing her off like that."

Sarry giggled and then quickly turned it into a cough, and Dorcas couldn't look at her.

Aunt Lizzie took their silence for agreement. "Now, I'm saying this for your own good, Dorcas. I promised your mammi that I'd look out for you while she was gone."

Something she could only describe as a muffled snort came from Sarry. Deciding she'd best get Aunt Lizzie moving before they both burst into laughter, she dropped her dishcloth and moved to Lizzie's side.

"That's so nice of you." She took Aunt Lizzie's arm. "Let me walk out with you. I know you don't want to be on the road when the light is starting to fade."

That got her moving, and Dorcas held the door and ushered her to her buggy. Unfortunately, Aunt Lizzie had something else to say.

Settled in her seat, she picked up the lines and paused, pinning Dorcas with a severe look. "You take my advice. Bring an end to that girl's visit. Her onkel needs to carry his own burdens."

Dorcas opened her lips to say she didn't find Katie a burden, but Aunt Lizzie was already backing the buggy out. Maybe that was just as well. With a quick wave, she scurried back into the house.

"I was afraid I'd start to laugh..." The

words dried up on her lips when she reached the kitchen, where Sarry still stood at the sink.

Sarry wasn't laughing. She stared at the soapy water, her hands hanging limply. Her lower lip stuck out, and she looked like she was going to burst into tears.

Dorcas rushed to her. "Sarry, was ist letz? What's wrong?"

Sarry shook her head, her face stuck in the stubborn expression that meant she was upset or afraid.

Dorcas put her arms around her. "Komm, tell me. Is it Aunt Lizzie?"

If anything, her lower lip protruded even more, and tears filled her eyes.

"It is, ain't so?" She held her more tightly, feeling a familiar exasperation with her great-aunt.

After a long moment, Sarry nodded.

Dorcas squeezed her gently and thought about what she'd like to do with Aunt

Lizzie. Maybe a piece of tape across her mouth would help her keep from hurting folk with her words. She put her cheek against her sister's and whispered in her ears.

"Better to tell me than to hold on to it."

Sarry held back from her for another moment. Then the words burst out. "She said I should be ashamed."

"Whatever for? You haven't done anything to regret." She tried not to think that Aunt Lizzie was the one to be ashamed.

"She said I should go. She said I made it hard for you."

"That's foolishness!"

Dorcas squeezed her sister tightly, and this time Sarry squeezed back. Dorcas struggled to find the words that would make this all right. Sarry's understanding was about like Matty's, and she tried to think what he would respond to.

"Listen, remember when you moved in?" She stroked back the hair that had slipped from under Sarry's kapp, curling in the dampness from the dish water. "It was right after Matty was born. You were so much help. I couldn't have managed without you. And when Luke passed… I needed you so much." The lump in her throat made it hard to speak. "You know, ain't so?"

Sarry's gaze seemed to search her face. Then she smiled, and it was like the sun coming out.

"I know," Sarry said, giving her characteristic nod. "I know."

Dorcas held her sister close. From the time Sarry was born, Dorcas had accepted Sarry as her responsibility, and she loved her as much as she loved her own kinder.

Her thoughts moved to Aunt Lizzie, and she had to slam the door on them.

The words she'd spoken such a short time ago seemed to ring in her ears.

If the gut Lord had sent Aunt Lizzie to help her build patience, He surely thought she needed it desperately.

Jacob slowed the horse and buggy he'd rented from the woman who ran the Amish Inn. He suspected James and his wife would have invited him to stay with them, but there was no reason to impose on them. It was better to be someplace where he was a customer, not a guest, now that he was back in Lost Creek. Better for them, and better for him, as well.

There was the lane to Dorcas's place. He turned in, wishing he'd taken time to call and let them know his plans. But this visit to Lost Creek was as much business as anything else, and they didn't need to be involved with it. The fact that he planned to check up on his niece was minor.

By the time he'd gotten down and hitched the horse to the hitching rail, Dorcas was coming out the back door. He'd expected her to look surprised, but his arrival didn't seem to have disrupted that calm serenity of hers.

"Wilkom, Jacob. It's nice to see you. Please, come inside."

She held the screen door open, and he went in, carrying the bag in which he'd packed some of Katie's clothes. She certain sure hadn't packed much when she left. Too eager to get away, he guessed, but now she wanted more.

Once they were both inside, he held the bag out for her. "This is for Katie. I brought the things she asked for as best as I could figure them out. She'll need some other things maybe, but Cousin Ada wasn't much help." His irritation with Ada showed clearly in his voice, he knew.

"Denke," she said, looking surprised. "That's wonderful kind of you."

Didn't she suppose he was smart enough to think a teenager would want a change of clothes?

"Cousin Dorcas..." Katie skipped in, followed by the youngest boy, who seemed to have appointed himself her shadow. "Onkel Jacob—you're here!" Her face clouded ludicrously. "You don't want me to come home, do you?"

Jacob suppressed a chuckle. "No worries. I brought some of the things you asked for, and anything else I thought you might be needing by now." He handed the bag over to her.

"Ach, Onkel Jacob, what a good idea." She beamed, pulling the bag open to see what he'd brought. "My pink dress—just what I wanted for tonight." She stopped abruptly, looking like she wanted to slap her hand over her mouth.

"What's going on tonight?"

"Ach, I'm forgetting my manners." Dorcas pulled out chairs at the kitchen table, setting the coffeepot on the stove. "Komm, sit down."

Dorcas began slicing coffee cake. "You'll have some, won't you?"

"Just a slice, denke." Now, what were they both so upset about? He glanced from one to the other and asked his question again. "What's going on tonight?"

Dorcas put the plate of coffee cake in front of him without meeting his eyes. "We'll be going out before long. Sally King and her husband are having a picnic and singing for the teenagers tonight."

Jacob put down his fork without touching the coffee cake. "Katie is too young, as I think you know. She's not ready for rumspringa yet."

And Katie had probably told Dorcas about the blowup they'd had over Katie wanting to go to some such thing in Bellport.

Chin tilted up, Dorcas looked him straight in the eye. "You agreed to let Katie stay for a visit. You didn't set any particular boundaries, ain't so?"

Katie, to do her credit, wasn't bursting into speech. Apparently she thought she should let Dorcas fight this battle.

His jaw tightened. "I didn't think I needed to. I thought you understood the usual restrictions for young people not quite old enough for rumspringa. It looks as if I was wrong."

If that troubled Dorcas, she didn't let it show.

"Some of the rules regarding rumspringa vary from one church district to another. It happens that the bishop agreed with Sally King's idea to invite the younger teens for a get-together. After all, it's warm for picnics outdoors, and nice for the fourteen- and fifteen-year-olds to get to be friends now that they're out of school."

Dorcas obviously thought that was a good enough reason to let Katie do something she must have known he wouldn't like. But before he could say anything more, Dorcas smiled, her cheerful expression distracting him.

"Ach, Jacob, what do you think is going to happen at a well-chaperoned event like this? You must have been a wild teenager if you got up to mischief at a singing."

He saw Katie sent her a startled glance, as if even she wouldn't have thought of saying that.

"I... That's not the point. Anyway, I don't know these youngers. How can I tell what they might get up to? As for the chaperones—"

"You don't need to worry about the chaperones."

"How do I know that?" He felt his fingers crumbling the coffee cake and put it down hurriedly.

"Because I'm one of the chaperones. And if that's not enough, you can be one, as well."

Now she was volunteering him for that very unwelcome job? A little voice seemed to whisper that the job shouldn't be unwelcome if he was as dedicated to bringing up Katie as he said.

"I have things to do tonight." He realized the battle was lost, but he wasn't quite ready to give up yet.

"Business, I suppose? Why did you come? And why are you driving the horse and buggy from the Amish Inn?"

"Do you always ask so many questions?" He frowned at her, trying to keep himself from smiling at the whole ridiculous argument.

"It seemed a gut idea if I wanted the answers. Komm, now. There can't be anything you have to do tonight that is so important. Are you going with us? I plan to drive, and you can follow us."

"Certainly not." He heard a gasp from Katie. "I will drive the two of you." He suspected if he looked at his niece, she'd be grinning. "And don't think that means that I agree with this foolishness. I don't!"

Chapter Five

Once they were on the way, with Katie dressed in the pink dress she was so fond of, Dorcas tried to decide if she had handled the situation right. She glanced toward the other two occupants of the buggy.

One thing was clear. Katie's choice of the coral pink had been a good one. It brought out the color in her cheeks and made her blue eyes sparkle. She was clearly excited about the evening ahead.

As for Jacob… Well, she still found it difficult to tell what he was thinking.

He had a talent for maintaining that stiff facade that didn't give anything away.

It wasn't all facade, she decided. His strong bone structure and square jaw added to the impression of a firm, decided disposition. Maybe he wasn't as stern as that made him look, but so far she hadn't seen any indication of it.

Jacob turned his head just then and caught her gaze.

"Is it much farther? Katie's too excited to give me directions. If she knows them."

"She was here on Sunday for worship and again yesterday to help the twins get things ready. She could probably direct you here without any problems."

Did that please him, or make him more annoyed? She had no idea. The men of the Lost Creek settlement were easy to interpret in comparison. She'd known most of them as long as she could remember, and known their families, as well.

That made a difference, for sure. She could pick out the tendencies that ran in families—a quick temper, a gift for animals, slow speaking and deliberate thinking—all those traits popped up here and there, reminding her of a father or a brother at times. But Jacob was a closed book. She knew little about his family except for a few things Mary Ann had said in her few letters. Mary Ann never had been much of a letter writer.

She brought her attention back to the road, resolving to stop thinking about Jacob so much. He'd really give her a hard time if she missed the turn after what she'd said.

"The next lane coming up on the left is the King place," she told him, and the horse turned in as he touched the lines.

The sun sent slanting beams across the broad fields, making them glow with the golden green of spring. The trees hadn't started to leaf out yet, but there was an indefinable air of spring about the scene. Maybe it was the freshly turned fields ready for planting, or splashes of color here and there from some of the early spring flowers.

"Nice place," Jacob commented, surprising her.

"Yah, it is. Aaron has two older brothers, and the family has been here as long as we have. Checking out the interconnections of the King family could take anyone a year, I think."

"Related to you?"

He did seem to be mellowing. He was willing to talk a little, or trying to, at least.

"Distant cousins, I guess you'd say. A couple of generations ago, somebody intermarried. But Sally is a good friend. We went through rumspringa together."

Maybe she shouldn't have mentioned that, Dorcas thought. But he had to get used to the word in connection with Katie at some point. She was growing up, whether he was ready for it or not.

"That's Aaron and his two oldest boys, setting up the volleyball court." Dorcas pointed to the flat area to the left of the barn. She probably didn't need to say that Sally and the twins were buzzing around the large picnic table. That was obvious.

"Stop, please," Katie cried. "I need to go and help the twins."

They came to a stop, and one of the boys raced over to take the horse and buggy from Jacob. Meanwhile Katie jumped to the ground and hurried to the twins. They grabbed her hands and tugged her toward the table, chattering away.

Dorcas accepted the hand Jacob extended to help her down, realizing he wasn't looking at her. His eyes were fixed on his niece instead. Wary, concerned… What did he think would happen to her at a singing?

He was overreacting, but she couldn't do anything about that. Still, her goal for the evening was clear—to see that nothing adverse occurred to raise trouble between Jacob and his niece. It was highly unlikely that anything would, but she couldn't help but be aware of his critical eyes looking for trouble.

The little cluster of adults came to meet them, and Dorcas made introductions. A few minutes later, Jacob was giving Aaron a hand with the volleyball setup. Dorcas sighed with relief. At least he was occupied for a time. She joined Sally and began setting out paper plates and napkins.

"So that's the man," Sally said.

"That's him," Dorcas murmured, not wanting to be caught staring at him, but curious to see how Jacob compared with the men of Lost Creek.

"He'd be good-looking if he smiled a bit more," Sally said.

Dorcas couldn't help but giggle. "Why don't you tell him so?"

"Me?" Sally put on a horrified look, but laughter underscored her words. "I wouldn't dare. He looks like he wouldn't appreciate any advice, no matter how well intended."

"That's true enough." She'd already seen that.

Apparently the volleyball court was ready. Aaron sent a ball across the net right at Jacob, saying something laughingly. At first she thought Jacob was going to ignore it, but then he sent it barreling back at Aaron. A little teasing, a little laughter, and then the game was on. The other fathers who were chaperoning joined in, and then the kids. More kids arrived, and everyone was swept into the game.

Reminding herself that she was here to help, not play games, Dorcas helped carry jugs of lemonade and iced tea out to the picnic table, following Sally.

"Are you going to call them to supper at a particular time?" Dorcas asked. "Or just let it happen as they get tired of playing?"

Sally was an organizer, and Dorcas knew that letting things happen wasn't her way. It was predictable that she was the one who'd come up with this idea in the first place.

"I want to get the singing started by six thirty, so they'll have to eat before that," Sally said. "If they lag behind, we'll need to remind them."

"How long do you plan for the singing?"

Usually the teen groups went on for two hours, but Sally had mentioned shortening the time for the younger ones.

"I'd think we can let them sing for forty-five minutes or so, then have drinks and dessert, a few more songs, and still get them out by eight or eight thirty. Sound good?"

Dorcas nodded. "That should be plenty of time." For the grown-ups, if not for the teens, she thought, and resisted the urge to suggest making it shorter just because it might be better as far as Jacob was concerned.

Sally reached out to touch her hand, as if thinking she needed assurance. "You're anxious that nothing goes wrong, ain't so?"

"That's certain sure." It was good to know that Sally understood, but they'd been friends for so long that they could almost see what the other person was thinking. “So far Jacob and Katie seem to be doing pretty well, but I don’t want to press it.”

As more kids arrived, most of the fathers retired from the game, gathering around the cold drinks. Holding a second cup, Jacob drifted over to her.

“Iced tea okay?” he asked, holding a cup out to her.

“Fine. Denke,” she said, surprised that he’d made the gesture. Dorcas watched the game, keeping an eye on Katie. She assumed Jacob was doing the same, but when she glanced his way, she found he was looking at her with a slight frown. Before she could ask what he’d found to frown about, he spoke, using the words she would have used.

“Was ist letz? What’s wrong?”

She blinked, taken by surprise. “That’s

what I was going to ask you. Katie seems to be fine."

He shook his head slightly. "I meant with Sarry. She seemed to be fretting about something when I tried to talk to her before we left."

How odd that it was the stranger who saw the cloud that Sarry was carrying around. She shouldn't say anything, but she couldn't deny it.

"Poor Sarry. She had a set-to with Aunt Lizzie yesterday."

"Who is Aunt Lizzie?"

Fortunate man, to have stayed clear of her. She shook her head, trying to still the negative words that wanted to spill out.

"Aunt Lizzie is actually my great-aunt on my mother's side. It's nothing to fret about, really. She likes to give folks advice, whether they want to hear it or not. So stay clear of her unless you want her to tell you all about how to run your business."

He shrugged. "Doesn't bother me. Lots of folks think they know stuff they don't. But what did she find to pick on Sarry about?"

Clearly he wasn't going to let go of the subject. Jacob seemed to have a protective streak for Sarry, despite how little he knew her. Maybe he had others close to him like Sarry.

"Ach, it was nothing. Please, just forget about it. I'm sure Sarry will by tomorrow."

"Will you?"

The man was persistent—too persistent.

"I should, that's certain sure. I know how Aunt Lizzie is. But Sarry—" Her throat grew tight. "My sister is very precious to me. To all of us. The idea of telling her that she was a burden to me—"

She shook her head, trying to dismiss the thought. "Please, forget I said anything."

"I won't go around talking about it," he said, as if she'd accused him of being a blabbermaul. "But I'm sure people you love aren't a burden."

The words surprised her, coming from him. Was he thinking of the young wife he'd lost? Before she could find any response, the game ended and the picnic table was swarmed by hungry kids.

Jacob stood back and watched while Dorcas and the other mothers pressed food on the noisy group of kids and tired adults. Most of the men, he suspected, were like him, working hard every day, but not at something that required the speed of volleyball. Still, they were laughing.

He'd planned to be watching Katie during all this mixing, but she seemed more interested in the twins and the other girls than in any of the boys.

Besides, he kept getting distracted by Dorcas, maybe because she seemed different from most of the women he knew. Being left a widow so young would have been difficult, especially with three children.

She had plenty of family support, he knew, but it must have taken a lot of courage and perseverance on her part to come through it so well. The loss of a spouse was devastating, as he knew only too well.

His situation was different, he reminded himself. Very different. He'd certain sure never be telling Dorcas about that.

Someone shoved a plate of food into his hands, and he looked up to see that it was Aaron.

"Better eat up," he said, grinning. "Sally

will be moving them on to the next thing before you know it."

"She has a schedule, does she?" He bit into a piece of fried chicken and realized how hungry he was. He could eat a whole platter of it.

"Sally's a born organizer," her husband said. "But in this case we promised the bishop and the ministers we'd have them home early. It's the first time we've done this, so we don't want to put a foot wrong."

"Yah, I can see that. Seems to be going well." He hadn't liked the idea to begin with, but it seemed to be okay. Just harmless fun and games. And it was nice to see Katie so happy.

Maybe Dorcas had something in her idea that Ada had been keeping her too close. Not that Ada would ever admit it. According to Ada, everything was either Katie's fault or his fault.

Well, he knew now that he'd have to find someone else to look after her before he could bring her home. Maybe he should be thanking Dorcas for her involvement, but he didn't feel that grateful.

Meanwhile Aaron lingered, looking as if there was something else on his mind—something he wanted to say.

"You know, Dorcas and Sally have been friends forever. We know her as well as anyone. You can trust Dorcas with Katie."

"Yah. I know," he mumbled, and then realized it was true. His initial mistrust of Dorcas was long gone. Yah, he could trust her, but Katie was his responsibility. A man couldn't just turn his responsibility over to someone else, not if he had any sense of honor.

He hadn't really thought Sally and Aaron would be able to keep to their timetable, not with this bunch of rowdy young ones. But sure enough, they were swept toward the barn right on schedule.

Dorcas glanced at him, and he walked over to join her. "We go in before the kids, and they'll shake hands with the adults before they start on the singing. Then we can relax a little bit." Her smile flashed. "They can't get into mischief while they're sitting on opposite sides of the table and singing, ain't so?"

He sent his thoughts back to those days that seemed so long ago. "Yah, I guess."

He remembered a certain amount of jostling to get seated opposite his special someone. He seemed to see Teresa—her dark brown eyes watching him, the soft curve in her cheek, looking no more than sixteen.

If they hadn't been so eager to marry… He stopped that thought before it could get going. There was no use in thinking about what might have been.

Dorcas seemed to be conscious of his distraction as she led him into the barn, but she didn't speak, and they joined the row of adults standing to one side of the door.

It was still light outside, but darkness had crept into the barn. Aaron had hung battery lanterns from hooks to cast light throughout the indoor area, where the tables they used for the Sunday lunch were lined up in a long row with benches on either side.

And here came the young people—the boys first in a long line, most of them looking serious and very young. The girls when they came were more composed, shaking hands with each adult and murmuring a greeting. He'd forgotten that about kids this age.

Soon they were seated on the benches,

the lanterns above showing up the serious young faces. Beyond the tables, shadows gathered in the corners. Chairs had been set up for the adults. Dorcas touched his sleeve and indicated the chairs.

Familiar hymns came first, each one started by a tall blond boy who seemed to fancy himself in the role of leader. Everyone knew the words, and everyone sang, even the adults joining in. Sally leaned over, squashing Dorcas, to whisper to Jacob that they'd do some lighter songs later, led by one of the girls.

"How light?" he whispered to Dorcas once Sally had sat back.

Her eyes twinkled. "Not anything from the Top Ten, I'm sure. Probably country western or folk songs."

She was probably waiting for a protest from him, but he didn't oblige, just shrugged. Even some of the men in the shop liked to sing that sort of music while they worked.

It had been some time since he'd sung with anyone except in worship, and he'd forgotten what a pleasure it could be. Aaron had put his arm across the back of Sally's seat, his hand touching her shoulder. His face lit when he looked at her, as if they were fifteen again.

Jacob, suddenly conscious of watching them with something like envy, looked away quickly. His gaze met Dorcas's, and that sense of envy increased. His hand moved, touching hers where it was partly hidden between the seats by her skirt. He thought he felt a flow of warmth from her. He told himself he should pull his hand away, but it took him several more seconds to manage it.

If he had waited for the right woman—but he hadn't, and he had to live with the results. He couldn't look for happiness anywhere else, not with the painful truth he had to keep hidden.

Dorcas busied herself helping Sally set out the desserts and drinks that various parents had sent—recognizing one person's chocolate peanut butter oatmeal cookies, and another's lemon cheesecake squares. Unfortunately, that didn't serve to keep her thoughts away from what had just happened.

She hadn't expected her reaction to Jacob's touch on her hand. Or the fact that he had not withdrawn it instantly.

Had he felt the warmth she had? It was impossible to tell from his face. His expression was the same as if he'd just touched the leg of the chair.

And what was she doing, anyway, thinking like that? Jacob wasn't interested in her. According to Katie, he wasn't interested in love. Nor was she.

They'd both loved and lost. That should be the end of it, but her hand still tingled with warmth.

The singers came to the end of a rousing "She'll be Coming Round the Mountain," and the scraping of chairs announced they were on their way. Sally gave the table a final look and stepped back.

"Best not get between them and the cold drinks," she said.

"Not me. They won't even look up long enough to see the crescent moon."

"Ach, well, we were probably the same. They're interested in food and each other—not necessarily in that order."

So true, Dorcas thought. This was the point during a singing with the older teens that some observation was important, just in case any of them decided to slip away. That shouldn't happen with this group, she'd think, but she'd still try to keep an eye on Katie.

The kids poured out through the wide barn doorway and swarmed the table. "Just like a horde of locusts," Sally said as the other adults joined them.

Aaron came up to join his wife. "Just have something yourselves and wander around a bit, so they remember we're here."

"You should know all about the shadowed nooks, ain't so, Aaron?" someone called out, making the others laugh.

"I'm not answering that when my own daughters are here," he retorted. "We'll call them back for a few last songs in about fifteen minutes, yah, Sally?"

Sally nodded, and Dorcas saw Jacob watching Katie. He'd probably want to skip out early, and she braced herself to argue the point when she saw him coming toward her.

To her surprise, he didn't mention it,

just came and stood next to her for a moment.

"Anywhere in particular we should keep an eye on?" Once again his gaze was fixed on Katie.

She shrugged. "Let's just take a walk around the barn. We don't have any serious sweethearts here, so it shouldn't be a problem."

Jacob fell into step with her, tilting his head back to take in the moonlit sky, then stumbling a little on the uneven ground.

"Careful," she said, catching his arm and chuckling. "You don't want to go back to work and have to explain a black eye."

"Not a chance." They rounded the side of the barn and walked a little farther before he spoke again. Then he stopped, looking down at her. "I didn't have time to mention it earlier, but I'm not planning to leave before Monday or Tuesday."

Her eyebrows lifted, but it was dark enough that he shouldn't notice. "How are they getting along without you for that long?"

"Reuben Fisher has been with me from the beginning. I decided he could take care of things while I'm away." He sounded just a little embarrassed, and she wondered if his face was red. He added hastily, "I'm just a phone call away if there's a problem."

"Yah, of course," she murmured, looking up at what she could see of him in the dark and wondering if her reaction to his one-man operation had influenced his decision. If so, he wouldn't admit it.

"I thought about what you said," he said, promptly proving her wrong.

That should teach her a lesson about

thinking she knew how people would react.

"This area is as good a place as any to look around for a site for a new plant," he added. "Nice town, plenty of Amish youth who might be looking for work." He hesitated. "Good people, too."

He was studying her face, she thought, though he probably couldn't see much in the shadows. The evening was very still, and to the west, the stars had begun to show, spangling the heavens.

Dorcas's breath seemed to catch in her throat, and she felt as if she couldn't move. The silence stretched between them, and neither of them seemed to want to break it.

Then Jacob took her elbow in a businesslike way. "We'd best finish our round or they'll be looking for us, ain't so?"

She nodded, still not sure she could

manage to speak. How foolish she'd been, so anxious about Katie's behavior at the singing, not wanting her to do anything to raise problems.

It looked as if her own behavior was what she should be worrying about.

Chapter Six

Dorcas bent over the rhubarb plants in the garden the next day, gently brushing the leaves back to see the size of the stalk. It was early, but the umbrella-shaped plants seemed ready to take over the garden. A good season for rhubarb, she thought, with visions of rhubarb pie.

"This one, Dorcas?" Sarry, a few feet away, squatted next to a six-inch stalk.

"Yah, looks good. Any bigger and it'll be the size of the boys' baseball bat."

She and Sarry exchanged grins, both knowing that Daad always said the bigger the better about his rhubarb. Dorcas didn't argue, but continued to pick hers while the stalks were still tender and fleshy. The same with asparagus. It was how it tasted that mattered, not how it looked.

Sarry pulled the rhubarb carefully and set it in the basket. Frowning a little, Dorcas glanced toward the house.

"I thought Katie was coming to help us. Do you know what she's doing?" Dorcas rubbed away the line between her brows, wondering again if she was the best person to deal with a teenage girl. Boys, she thought, were easy in comparison, and she understood boys.

Sarry wrinkled her nose. "Mopey."

Dorcas had to agree. Katie had seemed delighted about her first singing—in fact, she'd chattered about it all the way home. But this morning her mood had flip-flopped, and she'd been…well, distracted was probably the best word.

Stretching her back, Dorcas started to bend over the plants again when she heard the screen door open and close. Katie moved toward them, the usual lilt in her walk muted.

"Do you want me to do something in the garden?" she asked, skirting around the strawberry plants along the edge.

"Rhubarb," Sarry announced, holding one up.

Katie's nose wrinkled. "They're so sour."

Sarry smiled. "Needs sugar. That's all. Yummy, too."

Katie looked as if she didn't believe it, and her nose wrinkled again.

Dorcas pictured all three of the boys copying the expression and decided to stop it before it spread.

"You'll like it the way we fix it," she

said briskly. "See if you can find another one this size. We'll give a few to James and Anna."

Still pouting, Katie bent over the plants.

What was wrong with the girl? Other than being fifteen, that was? Maybe Katie needed a little reminder.

"Last night was fun, ain't so?"

Katie's smile came back, her eyes sparkling. "I wish we could do it all over again."

"I guess everybody loves a party." She kept her voice even, not wanting to scold. "But we can't let it spoil us for the ordinary things. Most days are ordinary."

For a moment, Katie didn't react. Then, as if just understanding Dorcas's meaning, she looked up with a horrified expression.

"I didn't mean… Ach, I'm sorry. Really." Sudden tears filled her bright blue eyes. "I love being here and helping you and everything. I'm sorry, Dorcas. I'm sorry, Sarry."

Sarry, who was closest to her, reached over the row of plants to give her a playful pat. "Okay," she said, grinning.

Katie took a long step over the intervening row of plants and threw her arms around Dorcas. "I didn't mean anything. I love being here." Her arms tightened. "Because of you...all of you."

"It's fine," Dorcas said, rubbing Katie's back gently. She was relieved that her gentle correction had worked so well, but a bit concerned, too. Whether she liked it or not, at some point Katie would have to go back to her uncle.

"Last night was fun," she went on. "I don't blame you for wishing for another."

"It wasn't *that*. I liked it, yah." Katie bent over another plant, her voice floating up uncertainly. "But I... I was wondering… Well, do you think I could ever be popular like the twins?"

Katie glanced at Sarry, who responded with a huge shrug, her shoulders up to her ears and her hands outspread.

Dorcas suppressed a chuckle, sure the child was perfectly serious. "The twins have known everybody here since they were born, so of course that makes a difference. You just concentrate on getting to know people. They'll like you, too, for sure."

Katie considered that for a moment, and then her face relaxed in a smile.

Dorcas couldn't help wondering how Jacob would have responded. Would he think Katie's reaction had proved that she wasn't ready for this much freedom? Or perhaps that Dorcas hadn't handled it well?

Shaking her head, she chased the thoughts away. She picked up the basket and considered the weight of it. Sarry and Katie's basket should be plenty for Anna's family, and hers would make a nice big dish of rhubarb sauce, the deep pink of the Valentine variety glowing.

And soon the strawberries would ripen, and they could have strawberry rhubarb pie. If anything tasted like spring more than that, she didn't know what it was.

"This should be enough for now." She hefted her basket. "You two take that one over to Anna's house. I told her we'd bring some to her as soon as it's ready."

Katie sparkled. "Maybe I can hold the baby, ain't so?"

"I'm sure Anna would be happy to have you hold him."

Most girls Katie's age were old hands with babies. But Katie acted as if she'd never held one…another big gap in her life with Cousin Ada, it seemed.

In a few minutes Sarry and Katie went down the lane together, swinging the basket between them, on their way to James and Anna's house.

Dorcas headed into the kitchen, intending to get the rhubarb washed and sitting in cold water until time to cook it. The kitchen seemed oddly empty with the boys at school and everyone else gone. Empty and quiet, letting her own thoughts finally return to the previous evening.

Unlike Katie, she wasn't worried about whether everyone had liked her or not. Thank goodness she had long since outgrown that stage. No, now her worries were centered around just one person.

How had those moments with Jacob happened? In fact, what had happened? Looked at in the clear light of day instead of in the moonlight, she suddenly felt that she had made something out of nothing.

What happened, really? A momentary touch, a gentle look? Nothing else. Nothing to get excited about. Certainly Jacob hadn't thought anything at all about it.

All my own imagination, she scolded herself. Was she going to start acting like a widow looking for another husband? The kind of woman other women looked sideways at?

Her face grew hot, and she pressed her palms against her cheeks. How foolish she was. The first time a man stirred some sort of feeling in her, and she was imagining a situation that didn't exist.

Enough of that. She grabbed the basket and started unloading it. Having a teenage girl added to her household was difficult enough, without letting her own emotions become entangled. She would forget about Jacob, the sooner the better.

* * *

Later, with a pot roast simmering slowly on the stove, Dorcas took a moment to sink down in the kitchen rocking chair and enjoy the rare moments of peace. The boys would be home from school shortly, and she'd expected Katie and Sarry back by now.

Still, it could be challenging to get away from Anna. With only the three little ones to talk to most of the day, she enjoyed adult company and probably didn't want to let go of them.

Even as she thought it, Dorcas heard the sound of a buggy coming up the road. Not the boys or Sarry and Katie, but someone was arriving. Maybe Jacob? Something seemed to squeeze her chest when she thought of him.

She went to the door, and her heart sank. Aunt Lizzie was back. Already. Dorcas had to remind herself of what she'd told Katie and the twins. Some people were meant to help us become patient. The Lord must think she needed a little extra help with that lesson.

By the time Dorcas reached the buggy, Aunt Lizzie was already complaining, it seemed.

"Where are those boys of yours? They should come out and deal with the horse and buggy when you get company."

Dorcas fixed a smile on her face as she reached up to help Aunt Lizzie down. "The boys aren't home from school yet, Aunt Lizzie. What brings you here?" She had to bite her tongue to keep from adding, *so soon.*

With Aunt Lizzie standing next to her, Dorcas suddenly realized that her great-aunt seemed to be shrinking. Aunt Lizzie wasn't the imposing figure she'd seemed when Dorcas was a child.

Be patient, Dorcas reminded herself.

Dorcas tied the horse to the hitching rail and took Aunt Lizzie's arm. "You'll come in, yah?"

"What about Sarry and that Katie, then?"

Aunt Lizzie might be showing signs of age, but her tongue was as sharp as ever.

"I sent them over to Anna's with some early rhubarb. I'll be glad to pick some for you, if you like."

Aunt Lizzie shook her head firmly. "Can't abide the stuff. Too sour for my taste."

Reminded of Sarry and Katie's joking, she smiled. But then she thought of Aunt Lizzie upsetting Sarry, who had no defenses against sharp tongues, and the smile disappeared entirely.

As they went into the kitchen, the desire to speak about it became too strong to be ignored. "Maybe it's best if you don't see Sarry just now. You know you upset her the last time you talked."

For a moment her great-aunt just stared at her, and then the color came up in her face. Her gaze shifted away from Dorcas.

"I don't know what you mean." The words weren't very convincing.

"The last time you were here," Dorcas repeated. "You said something to Sarry—"

"I believe in straight talking," Aunt Lizzie interrupted. "If folks don't like it, that's too bad."

Aunt Lizzie was still avoiding her eyes, and Dorcas took a firmer grip on her temper.

"You told Sarry that she was a burden to me. That's not true." She remembered how she'd tried to comfort Sarry, and her heart twisted. The words Jacob had used came into her head.

"I love Sarry. Someone you love is never a burden."

"Well! Anyone can see you have enough to do with your own fatherless kinder. I was only trying to help."

"I'm sure you were." At least, she hoped so.

Aunt Lizzie shook her head, ignoring Dorcas's words. "As if you didn't have enough to do with your own family, you go taking in that Katie Unger—a girl who ran away from her own home and got into who knows how much trouble. You bring her into your home where she can influence your own kinder. What would your parents say?"

Dorcas's head was spun with unanswered questions. How did Aunt Lizzie know about Katie running away? She'd been careful about what she said, and surely neither James nor the kinder would say anything to Aunt Lizzie, of all people.

Dorcas grasped her tumbling thoughts. No matter how Lizzie had found out or who she told, it couldn't change what Dorcas did.

"I'm sure Mamm and Daadi will be pleased to know that I've extended a welcome to the child of my cousin," she said firmly. "Mary Ann was very dear to all of us."

She took a deep breath and reminded herself again of what she'd told the kinder about difficult people. Aunt Lizzie was difficult, all right, and Dorcas certain sure hadn't exhibited a lot of patience today. Maybe that *was* why the good Lord kept giving her opportunities to practice it.

Dorcas took her great-aunt by the arm and gently guided her toward the table. "I appreciate your concern, Aunt Lizzie, but everything is fine." She pulled out a chair, but Lizzie shook her head.

"I can't stay. I'm on my way to see Ethel Fisher." She turned toward the door and then looked back. "I just felt it my duty to speak to you, Dorcas. With your parents away, you need to be careful."

She considered a couple of replies to that and finally just shook her head. Aunt Lizzie wasn't going to change her ways because of anything Dorcas said.

They walked together out to the buggy, and just before climbing to her seat, Aunt Lizzie paused. Quite suddenly, she put her hand against Dorcas's cheek. A struggle seemed evident on her face.

Finally she gave Dorcas a little pat and turned to the buggy. Gathering up the lines, she shook her head. "I don't want to see you get hurt, Dorcas. That's all. You'll be better off staying away from those Ungers."

Before Dorcas could ask what she

meant, Aunt Lizzie had started off. Dorcas stood for a moment, looking after her. What on earth did Aunt Lizzie mean? Was she referring to Katie or Jacob or both? Did she know something about the Unger family that Dorcas didn't?

Jacob drove down the blacktop road toward Dorcas's place. He'd had a long day and come to no conclusions, but he'd found several locations that seemed promising. And was he calling on Dorcas to get her opinions on his search or to check on Katie?

Either one was reasonable, wasn't it? He silenced the little voice in his mind that hinted there might be another reason.

Ahead of him, Sarry and Katie stood by the lane leading to James's house, waving to him. At least, Sarry was waving, a big grin on her face. Katie didn't look very enthusiastic. Problems?

He drew to a stop next to them. "Hop up. We can squeeze three on this seat."

Sarry grabbed the side of the buggy, hauling Katie along with her. "Denke. We like a ride, ain't so?" Sarry nudged Katie, and Katie nodded.

Something had happened to last night's enthusiasm. Was she anticipating that he'd find fault with her behavior? Or had there been some problem with Dorcas?

Before he could probe, the boys came hurrying down the path that led to the school, waving and yelling. At least, Matty was. The other two came along behind, Timothy scooping up the lunch box Matty had dropped. They walked alongside the buggy, with six-year-old Matty babbling all the time. It was easy to enjoy the youngest—he had no reservations about seeing Katie's uncle as a friend.

Silas, the middle boy, responded to his brother's chatter with a frown. "Stop it, Matty. Nobody wants to hear all that."

Matty looked ready to argue the point, but Timothy cut him off. "Take your lunch boxes to the kitchen. Matty, be sure you show Mammi your spelling paper."

Matty's smile vanished and he pouted, but he did scamper off to the kitchen, with Silas behind him.

"Trouble with spelling?" he asked lightly, but Timothy didn't respond. In fact, he eyed Jacob with something that looked like suspicion.

Jacob shrugged it off. What did he care what Dorcas's children thought of him? He had more important things to do. Hitching the horse to the rail, he walked quickly toward the phone shanty, feeling the need to talk to Reuben. Everything he'd seen today was beginning to scramble itself in his mind.

He'd talk to Reuben, and then he should sit down someplace quiet to make notes while things were fresh in his mind. That was the right way to approach a decision.

When he walked into the kitchen fifteen minutes later, he found Dorcas alone. She was bent over a heavy kettle on the stove, the heat turning her face rosy.

She replaced the lid. "Pot roast," she said. "You'll stay for supper, yah?"

He hesitated, lured by the tempting aroma, while his conscience suggested he do what he came to do and leave. Moving over to the counter, he put a twenty-dollar bill down.

"For the phone calls," he said, focusing on business first.

Dorcas looked shocked. “That’s not necessary. You…you’re more than wilkom. You’re our guest.” She looked at the money as if it was a snake that had popped up in her kitchen. Picking it up, she thrust it toward him. “Take it back, please.”

He put his hands behind him, determined to win this one. “You’d best keep it. Otherwise I’ll have to put it into Matty’s lunch box. Who knows what would happen to it then?”

She smiled. “You wouldn’t suggest that if you’d ever seen the inside of his lunch box when he gets home. I keep finding remains of things I didn’t send with him. It looks like the first graders never eat their own lunches.”

Jacob told himself he wasn’t remotely interested, but Dorcas’s eyes had the sparkle he always saw when she talked about her young ones. He couldn’t help smiling in return.

It was on the tip of his tongue to ask why Timothy didn't like him when he realized he didn't want to hear the answer. That wasn't any of his business, and Dorcas could easily resent his question. Better to leave it alone.

No sooner had he decided that, than Dorcas spoke. "Has Timothy been polite to you? Sometimes he acts as if he's..."

"Suspicious of me? I noticed. He's protective of you. That's natural."

She flushed, the color coming up in her cheeks as it had when she'd bent over the pot roast. "I guess that's true. I'm sorry."

He shrugged. "Forget it. He's just trying to take his daad's place, ain't so?" The words were a surprise to him—he hadn't realized he'd even considered Timothy except as part of a cluster of young ones. But it had to be true. He knew how he'd felt when his father died. "Don't let it worry you."

"Worry comes with the territory." Dorcas wiped her eyes with the tea towel she held. "I can remember my grandmother saying that a mother is only ever as happy as her saddest child."

That had never occurred to him, but the truth of the saying landed in his heart, making him think of Katie. If anyone asked him, he would have said that it was natural that Katie was unhappy—she'd lost the people she loved best in the world. But that was several years ago now.

His brother had entrusted Katie to his care. What had he done to even attempt to fill that gap? Providing a roof over Katie's head and food to eat wasn't the whole job. Was it possible he might have missed the most important thing?

Chapter Seven

It wasn't until a bit later that Dorcas realized Jacob hadn't answered her question about supper. And that the twenty-dollar bill was still lying on the counter. She picked up it and put it in the pottery jar on the shelf, her usual spot for small items she didn't know what to do with.

As for supper, what difference did it make? The pot roast would easily stretch. She popped a couple more potatoes into the kettle and wiped her hands. It could simmer until supper time.

She glanced around the kitchen. Everything was in order, and she'd best check on what was happening outside.

Timothy was putting the pony's harness on. For a moment she didn't understand. Had she forgotten some errand she should run?

Then she realized what was happening. Timothy was showing Katie how to harness the pony to the pony cart. Katie stood opposite to him, watching intently, the pink dress she wore bringing out the rosiness in her cheeks.

Jacob stood a few feet away, also watching, along with Sarry. She was clutching Matty, who obviously wanted to help.

Jacob must have suggested Timothy teach Katie. She couldn't see any other reason for his standing quietly watching. Studying his face, Dorcas tried without success to decipher his feelings. Was this connected to what he'd said about Timothy trying to fill his father's shoes? But how could it be?

"I'll help!" Matty, breaking away from Sarry's control, darted forward, clearly intending to join the fun. Dorcas grabbed him and pulled him back against her.

"They don't need your help," she said, giving him a squeeze.

"Ah, Mammi, I can show Katie as good as Timothy can. I'm good at harnessing, ain't so?" He twisted his head to look up at her, so that she saw his chubby cheeks and blue eyes from a different angle.

"You're not bad." She tickled him under the chin, making him giggle. "But I'm guessing Jacob gave the job to Tim."

Matty pouted, but then he nodded. "I guess."

"Yah, I did," Jacob said, hearing them. "Maybe there's something else you can show Katie."

"That's right. She doesn't know anything about the chickens, and you can teach her to gather the eggs," Dorcas agreed.

It seemed Jacob was showing more understanding of the kinder than she'd expected. First his surprising insight into Timothy, and now this. Maybe he'd actually forgotten his precious business for a moment.

"Now you do that side," Timothy said, gesturing to Katie. "Go ahead, just like I did."

The tip of Katie's tongue poked from the corner of her mouth as she focused. "This one first, yah?" She picked up the buckle tentatively.

"That's right. Go ahead." Timothy was just about as focused as Katie was, and once she had buckled it correctly, he blew out a breath. "Gut job! Now the next one."

Once she'd seen Katie reach for the

right buckle, Dorcas glanced at Jacob. "I hope they asked for your permission before starting this, Jacob."

"As a matter of fact, it was my idea." He looked at her as if daring her to object.

She tried not to betray surprise. She'd hoped maybe Jacob himself might want to teach her, but this was even better. He was trusting her son with the job.

"Denke," she said quietly. "It's gut for him."

"I hope so."

She caught a touch of apprehension in his face.

"What could happen?" Even as she said the words, Katie flipped a rein out of her way, and it smacked against the mare's rear.

Jacob started forward, but she touched his arm to stop him.

"It's okay. Sadie didn't even feel it. If

she could put up with my three learning to drive, she can cope with Katie."

"Yah, she can," Sarry, overhearing them, put in. "Not Zion," she added.

Jacob looked confused, obviously scouring his memory for an Old Testament character.

Dorcas's lip twitched. "Zion is Silas's goat. My husband brought him home for Silas when Matty was born."

Matty wiggled in her grasp. "Mammi says that Daadi thought Silas should have a baby goat to look after. Just like Timothy helped watch the baby. Me, I mean," he added.

Jacob's face relaxed in a smile. "I figured that."

Relieved, Dorcas caught Sarry's eye. "Sarry and I better get on with supper. You will stay, yah?" She lifted her eyebrows in a question.

He nodded. "So long as you keep that

twenty dollars. I must have eaten that much at least."

"I wasn't counting," she said, pleased when his smiling gaze met hers. Poor Jacob. If he only looked that way most of the time, he'd be a lot easier to get along with.

Dorcas reminded herself that it wasn't any of her business, except as it affected Katie. Still, it was much more pleasant to see him smile.

She and Sarry headed for the house, and Dorcas stopped by the hitching rail to look back. Timothy and Jacob were leading the pony and cart into the paddock with Katie sitting in the driver's seat.

All was well, but a faint uneasiness slid along her nerves. Dorcas knew exactly what had caused it—Aunt Lizzie, with her confusing warnings about the Unger family. She'd been trying to forget what Lizzie had said, but it still clung like a burr.

What could possibly make Jacob an unsuitable person for her family to know? Something about his past? Some issue in his business?

That actually seemed more likely. It was difficult for an ambitious businessman to balance the line between Amish principles and success. And from what she'd heard, Jacob was very successful.

She shook her head, following Sarry into the kitchen. Jacob's business had nothing to do with them. She knew very little about it, and that suited her just fine.

Jacob had Charlie Downs drop him at Dorcas's brother's house the next day. They'd had a long day, driving past Millvale in Jacob's effort to check out every possibility, and he was beginning to wonder if this expansion idea was any good at all.

There seemed some problem everywhere he looked. Maybe he'd be better off expanding his existing facility.

"Denke, Charlie." He slid out of the car. "You'll pick me up at eight tomorrow, yah?"

Charlie nodded. "Should get you back home about noon, then." He accepted the money Jacob held out to him. "Hope you'll be back soon." His weathered face wrinkled in the smile that made him so likable. "We're getting to like having you."

Jacob nodded, wondering if that was true. At least Dorcas and her family had warmed up. He wasn't sure why that mattered to him, but it did.

A tiny voice at the back of his mind suggested he knew perfectly well that it was Dorcas herself who seemed to matter, but he slammed the door on that idea. Whether he'd been right or wrong in what he'd done when he learned of his wife's death, there was no going back now. He was stuck with it, and it put up a wall between him and any normal life with a wife and children.

James, Dorcas's brother, came out of his barn, spotted Jacob and came toward him with a welcoming smile.

"Hey, Jacob. How's your search going?"

He seemed as friendly as ever, and Jacob was relieved to see it. He wanted some information, maybe even advice, from James, and he thought he could rely on him for an honest opinion.

"Not bad, but not good, either. I thought maybe I could talk it over with you."

"Sure thing." James glanced toward the house and then shook his head. "We'll be overrun with the young ones if we go in the kitchen. Let's go in the barn and pull up a hay bale to sit on."

They walked through the center door of the Dutch-style barn, and James pulled a couple of bales from the hay mow.

"Now, have a seat and tell me all about it. I don't know much about your business, but I do know the area."

"Thing is, I've seen a lot of possibilities, but nothing that was really right. And I don't know enough about the communities to be sure my business would be welcomed."

James nodded, and Jacob could see that it wasn't a new idea to him. "Yah. There's been talk."

"I figured that." He'd hoped it wouldn't get started already, but that had been futile. "It's okay to run a gut business but not to be too successful, ain't so?"

James grinned. "That's the gist of it,

I guess. And there's some who wondered what effect it might have on the youngers. Will they get to wanting computers and electric and all that?"

"Not from me," he said promptly. "We use computers only for measurement and design of parts we make for Englisch factories. They're like any measuring device to us, but we use them because the company we sell to insists. The measurements have to be more precise than we'd get any other way."

"Gut." James chuckled. "And let's face it…teens can get their hands on computers and cell phones if they want to. I did, and I turned out all right. They don't need your help to find a computer. We just have to make sure that by the time they're ready to join the church, they don't want to bother with them."

Jacob found he was relaxing. He should have known that James would be as sensible as his sister was. "That's certain sure." He hesitated. "I don't want any gossip reflecting on Dorcas and your family, that's all."

"Have you been listening to Aunt Lizzie?" James said, grinning. "If there's gossip around, she'd be in the middle of it."

"I figured that from what Katie and her friends have to say." Again he paused, afraid of seeming too interested in Dorcas.

"You're wondering how Dorcas puts up with it, ain't so?" James didn't seem to have his inhibitions. "Thing is, our Dorcas has a big heart. She can't seem to keep from trying to help people, even if it causes problems for her. That's just who she is."

That, Jacob thought, was a pretty good insight for a younger brother. James and Dorcas were closer than many brothers and sisters, he'd guess, and what he'd said matched what Jacob himself thought. Dorcas was a special person, and the last thing he'd want was to hurt her in any way.

So it was just as well that he was headed for home tomorrow.

Dorcas came into the kitchen to find Katie in a tizzy. She seemed to be making biscuits, but from the way she was waving the spoon in the air, it looked as if the dough would land on the ceiling.

"Goodness, what are you doing?" Dorcas caught her hand. "If you want light biscuits, you have to handle the dough as little as possible, remember?"

"Please, Cousin Dorcas, please will you tell Onkel Jacob to stay for supper? He doesn't know I'm cooking tonight, and I want to surprise him. I'm doing the chicken pie with the biscuits on top, just like you showed me."

"Your uncle?" Her thoughts spun. "He's not here, is he? I thought he said something about leaving soon."

She realized how wrong she was even before Katie pointed toward the backyard and she heard Jacob's deep voice contrasting with the lighter tones of the boys' and Sarry's giggles.

"We'll ask him," she promised, even as she reminded herself that she'd probably been seeing too much of him. If she wasn't careful, the community would be buzzing about her.

Katie caught her arm. "Don't just ask, get him to stay. I want him to see how well I can cook now. I have to surprise him."

"He'll be surprised all right if you don't quit stirring those biscuits," Dorcas pointed out.

"Oh, no." Katie dropped the spoon. It bounced on the counter and then landed on the floor.

Katie's eyes filled with tears. "I've made a mess, and I wanted it to be special."

Dorcas scooped up the spoon. "It'll be fine. Just let the dough rest for a minute, and then you can top the casserole dish, okay? And I'll go convince him to stay."

"It's a secret, remember," Katie called after her as she headed out the back door.

If Jacob didn't hear that, he must be deaf. Dorcas avoided him and whispered to Sarry, telling her to keep an eye on Katie's cooking. Nodding, Sarry put her finger beside her nose and scurried inside. Apparently she already knew the secret.

She spared a moment to consider the differences between one teenage girl and three little boys. How had Mammi managed with her big family?

Shaking her head, she drifted over to the paddock, where Silas was showing his goat to Jacob. Or showing off, maybe. It was a sweet critter—most of the time, anyway, when it wasn't getting into her flowers.

"Zion ate all the poison ivy along the fence," Silas announced proudly as she joined them.

"That's gut," she said. "So long as you keep him away from the garden. I don't want him near the rhubarb and strawberry plants."

Silas frowned, shaking his head. "Mammi, you know I'm careful to keep him in the pen."

She gave him a quick hug. "Ach, I know."

"Silas tells me Zion is a dwarf goat. I don't think I've seen any of those at home." Jacob looked as if he'd be happy if he didn't see any more of them.

"Ach, you just need to get to know him. Dwarf goats are very playful and friendly." As if to prove Dorcas's words, Zion nibbled at Silas's hair and knocked his hat off before trotting over to the stacked boxes that made a climbing area for him. He scrambled up to the top, looking pleased with himself.

Jacob glanced at her. "Didn't you say your husband brought the goat home when he was just a little thing?"

Dorcas smiled, remembering that day. Silas had been a little mopey, probably missing the fact that he wasn't the baby any longer.

"Yah. He ran into somebody who was trying to find a home for it. The mother had rejected it, so it had to be fed with a bottle. Just like Matty," she added teasingly, making Matty grin.

Remembering what she was supposed to be doing, Dorcas turned to Jacob. "You'll stay for supper, won't you? It'll be ready before long."

But he was already shaking his head, and she was irrationally disappointed. And not just because of Katie.

"I'm heading for home early tomorrow, so I'd best go and pack up."

"Ach, you have to eat anyway, ain't so? Please stay."

She glanced up at his face and discovered that he was studying her as if memorizing what she looked like. Her heart lurched. "Will you? Please?" she stammered the words, very aware of the fact that his fingers had encircled her wrist.

"Something special about it?" His lips relaxed in a smile.

Dorcas grasped hold of herself. "It's a surprise, okay?"

His eyebrow lifted. “Can I guess what it is?”

“No,” she said hurriedly, convinced he’d guess correctly at the first try. “We’ll set a place for you.” Before he could say anything more, she scurried into the house.

Dorcas helped to get the table set while Katie and Sarry put the finishing touches to the meal, and when Katie rang the supper bell they all came in, including Jacob. Dorcas couldn’t stop a little tingle in her wrist at the sight of him, as if his fingers still touched her skin.

Katie’s eyes sparkled as she watched everyone digging into the casserole. When Jacob praised it, Katie sent a triumphant glance toward Dorcas.

“There, you see?” she announced. “I made it, Onkel Jacob. All by myself. I can cook now, and I’ve learned lots about taking care of a house.” She took a deep breath and then blurted out what she was thinking. "You can forget about finding someone to take care of me. I can move in and take care of you!"

Silence descended on the kitchen. Dorcas was as astounded as everyone else. Why hadn't she realized…?

Jacob dropped his fork on his plate. He glared at Dorcas, obviously blaming her.

"That's impossible," he said flatly. "Put that out of your mind right now."

He shot to his feet and strode out of the house.

Chapter Eight

For a long moment Dorcas just sat and looked at the screen door rattling in its frame. She could hardly believe he would just walk out that way. Katie was shedding angry tears, while the boys and Sarry just sat, staring.

If only Katie had told her what she'd intended… Well, there was no sense in expecting Katie to behave rationally when her uncle was just as bad. Muttering, Katie started to rise, apparently intending to stomp out herself.

"Komm, now, everyone. Sit down and

enjoy this delicious meal that Katie has prepared for us." She sent a firm look around the table. Everyone, including Katie after a moment's hesitation, stopped staring and started eating.

A few mouthfuls of food later, Katie said quietly, "It is gut, yah?"

"For sure," Dorcas said.

"Just like Mammi's, almost," Timothy said helpfully, and Dorcas smiled at him.

There was a moment's silence, and Dorcas waited for the inevitable question. It was Matty, of course, who asked it.

"Why did Jacob go out? Didn't he like it?" Matty took another mouthful and spoke around it. "It's gut."

"It wasn't that," Dorcas said, picking her words carefully. "I think it was Katie's idea of moving in with Jacob and taking care of him. Jacob was surprised."

"But surprises are good things," Silas protested. "Like presents."

Dorcas felt as if they'd had this conversation before.

"Sometimes a surprise doesn't seem good to the person being surprised. Remember when you fell out of the apple tree and broke your arm? You were surprised, but you weren't happy."

Silas considered that. "Yah. But afterward I had a cast and everybody wrote on it. And Grossdaadi made us chocolate ice cream. My favorite!"

She had to smile at his remembering. "It's best to wait and see what good things God can bring, even from something that seems bad at first."

"Well, Onkel Jacob could have looked more happy," Katie said. "I did make a gut supper."

Sarry grinned and raised a finger in the air. "One supper."

At first Katie didn't seem to understand what she meant. Then she managed a reluctant smile. "Maybe he wouldn't like it every night, I guess."

"Probably not." Dorcas sent a quick glance toward the door, beginning to wonder where Jacob had disappeared to. She'd think he'd realize by now that his manners needed some correction.

Matty gulped down half a glass of milk. "I was surprised the first day I went to school. It wasn't like I thought at all, but I liked it."

Timothy grinned. "That's because Silas told you the teacher would yell if you did something wrong."

"Yah, well, that's what you told me before my first day of school," Silas said.

"So naturally you did the same thing," Katie put in, beginning to get the hang of siblings. "I loved my first day of school. My mamm said I would, and I did."

Dorcas felt a small pang in her heart at the thought of Mary Ann. "She loved school when she was young, that's why."

Conversation had returned to normal, and she was grateful. She glanced at Katie, who smiled back, seeming to understand what she didn't say.

"Onkel Jacob did say that he liked my casserole, ain't so?" she asked again.

"He did," Matty declared. "I heard him."

"Yah, I did," Jacob spoke from the porch as he opened the screen door.

Dorcas felt a flush rising to her cheeks. How much had he heard? And had she said anything that she shouldn't have?

"Finish up now, everybody," she said. "And then we'll have some rhubarb pie."

"With strawberries in it?" Timothy asked hopefully.

"Silly," Katie said. "The strawberries aren't ripe yet."

"They're not, but I added some strawberry jam, just so there'd be a taste of strawberries in the pie."

"Yum." Timothy got up quickly and took his plate to the sink. "Come on, you guys, clear up. Don't you want pie?"

There was a general agreement to that, and Dorcas began cutting pie while Sarry put on the coffee and Katie carried the almost empty casserole dish to the sink. Jacob followed her with his plate, intercepting her.

"Let me have that last mouthful. It's too good to waste," he said, and Katie flushed and smiled.

Dorcas let out a thankful breath. Everyone was back to normal again, it seemed. Or mostly. It occurred to her that Jacob's gaze was still a little cool when it rested on her.

Well, what did it matter? It was his attitude toward Katie that was important, after all.

* * *

Jacob decided that the sooner he removed himself, the better. He'd reacted without thinking, and he'd hurt Katie's feelings as well as upset everyone else. Especially Dorcas, who'd been doing so much to help.

He hesitated as the kids swirled around him, the boys running outside to do their after supper chores while the others set about cleaning up from supper. He touched Katie lightly on the shoulder.

"I'm sorry." The words got caught in his throat, but he forced himself to go on. "I need to think about what you said and how it might work out. We'll talk about it soon. All right?"

Katie's sweet smile lit up her face. "Yah, okay." Sarry flicked a little dishwater toward her, and Katie turned back to her.

"I wash," Sarry announced.

"Only if you don't splash me," Katie said, grabbing a dish towel, the laughter back in her voice.

Relieved that Katie had forgiven him, Jacob turned to Dorcas. Was her gaze still wary? He couldn't be sure.

"Can I talk to you for a minute before I head back to the inn?"

She nodded without speaking, and they walked outside together. As if she'd suddenly realized he didn't have a buggy there, she glanced from the hitching rail to him.

"Do you want me to drive you back?"

He shook his head, embarrassed again—this time that he'd forgotten. "*Ach*, no. I spent so much time in the car today that I'd rather walk." He looked around, but no one was in sight. "Will you walk a little way with me?"

Dorcas seemed surprised, but she nodded. Together they skirted the colorful bed of daffodils and hyacinths and around a forsythia just reaching full bloom. The air was warm, and the scent of flowers drifted around them.

He stopped once he could be sure they weren't likely to be interrupted. He'd long since realized that it wasn't easy to have a private talk with anyone at Dorcas's house.

"You must have had a long search today." She gave him a questioning look. "Any success?"

He shrugged, finding it unexpectedly hard to focus on the expansion that had been filling his thoughts lately. "It's hard to say. Reuben and I have talked a lot about what we'd need, and nothing seems to be just right."

Her lips twitched. "My daad always says that buying property is like buying a horse. You never find anything that's exactly right, so you have to decide if you can fix it or do without it."

"Your father sounds like a wise man. That's the sort of advice my father would have given." For an instant he thought about having Daad here with him. His very presence had always been steadying.

"You miss him, yah?" Dorcas said, her voice soft.

"Yah." His voice had roughened, and he cleared his throat. "We could just expand where we are now, but we already have about as many people as we can manage in one place. Everyone needs to feel a part of it, and you can't do that if you get too big. And people start wondering about you. There's a feeling that Amish shouldn't make too much money."

He was very aware of the risks of looking too successful. Amish humility didn't combine with what the world called success.

He could see that he didn't need to tell her that… Dorcas had a way of understanding.

"Besides, if we do find a good place, maybe I'll put Reuben in charge of setting it up. Nobody understands the machinery as well as he does."

Funny that it had taken Katie running away for him to understand just how competent Reuben was.

He shook his head, knowing he'd gotten off track. "That wasn't what I wanted to say. You were exactly right about me. When Katie blurted out her plan I was too shocked to say anything else."

"Katie will get over it. In fact, she has already. As Sarry pointed out, you might like the chicken casserole, but not every single night."

She was smiling, her face tilted up to his, amusement shining in her eyes.

"That might be a little too much," he agreed. "Anyway, I'm grateful to you."

"There's no need to be. I tried to explain for my kids' sake, too. They need to understand that people react in different ways. Not everyone takes problems with a laugh."

For just a moment her lips trembled. He reached out to clasp her hands, and he thought he knew just what she was thinking.

"Was that what your husband was..." He stopped. That was going too far, to ask about her late husband. What was he thinking?

"It's all right." Her lips weren't trembling now, and they moved into a sweet, reminiscent smile. "Yah, that's what Luke was like...easygoing, taking things with a laugh and a joke whenever he could."

Completely different from him, obviously. He should go if he intended to get on the road early tomorrow. But somehow he couldn't let go of her hands, and he couldn't break away from her gaze.

"Mammi! Mammi!" Timothy was shouting, and she turned back in an instant, her attention no longer on him.

"What's wrong?" She sped toward the sound.

"It's Grossdaadi on the phone." Timothy rushed to her and grabbed her hands, pulling her. "He says the baby is here. He says it's twins. Boy twins!"

Dorcas raced her son back to the phone shanty, and Jacob realized he was forgotten.

Timothy, shaken out of his usual grown-up manner, jumped up and down beside her as Dorcas grabbed the phone, and a moment later the rest of the family poured out of the house and she was surrounded.

"Daadi?" She put her hand over her free ear. "Talk loud! Everyone is so excited they're making it hard to hear."

Her father's chuckle came through. "I can hear them. We're pretty excited here, too. Twins!"

There was so much she wanted to know that it was hard to get the questions out. "They're all right? Both of them? How much do they weigh? Boys, I hear. And Grace? How is she?"

"Wonderful," he boomed. "Your mamm will tell you more, that's for sure, but Grace hasn't stopped smiling. As for Ezra—his feet haven't touched the ground yet."

"And the babies?" She held her breath, picturing the two tiny boys in her mind.

"Fine, fine. Over five pounds, both of them, with a good pair of lungs. Listen."

He must have held the phone out because she heard a twittering of voices and then the unmistakable sound of hungry newborns.

Dorcas breathed a prayer of thanksgiving. Then, because Matty was pulling on her apron so hard it was about to come off, she turned away from the phone long enough to relay the news.

"I want to talk to them," Matty wailed as Sarry pulled him away, and she could hear Katie explaining.

"There, that's better." She pressed the phone against her ear again. "We're all so happy for them. What—"

"Dorcas, I must tell you something else. Your mamm will stay for another week or two, but I'm coming home soon. Tell your bruder, yah?"

"I will, but—"

"I have to hang up. Ezra wants the phone. I'll see you in a day or two."

He hung up before Dorcas could get out another question. Frustrated, she shook the receiver as if that would help. There was so much more she wanted to know, but it was useless expecting to hear it from Daad on the phone. He only used the telephone in emergencies, and as excited as he was, he probably didn't consider two healthy babies that. She'd have to wait for Mammi's call to hear all the details.

She stepped out of the phone shanty and into a hail of questions, most of which she couldn't answer. She waved her hands for quiet.

"Hush, now. Go and finish your chores, and we'll have a good long talk about your new cousins before you go to bed."

Several groans from the older boys greeted that, but they went off quickly enough. Timothy grabbed Matty's hand and pulled him along, and she could hear

Matty's excited questions all the way to the barn.

Then Sarry was waiting to give her an enormous hug. "Two new babies, yah? Two!"

"Yah, we have two new nephews." She kissed her sister's cheek, knowing how much Sarry loved babies. "We'll go down to Lancaster County to see them before long."

Sarry seemed content with that for now. "I'll make another little hat, yah?"

"Right. And we'll do another baby quilt, too." She thought of the sunny yellow crib quilt she'd finished and sent off with her mother. "A blue one this time."

Nodding, Sarry scurried into the house, probably to look for some soft blue yarn for the little hats she loved to crochet with Dorcas's help.

Dorcas turned, her gaze seeking out

Jacob, somehow wanting to share her joy. But he was nowhere in sight.

Katie slipped her arm around Dorcas's waist. "So nice. You have two new nephews."

"And you have two new cousins," she answered, squeezing her. "What happened to your uncle?"

Katie obviously had to drag her thoughts away from the babies. "He said he was going back to the inn. Getting an early start tomorrow." She stopped, looking shaken. "Did you…did you want me to go with him?"

"Ach, no. We agreed you'd stay here until things are settled." As for how that would happen, she still couldn't see the way clear.

Fortunately, Katie seemed content with her answer. "I'll go help the boys finish up." She hurried off toward the barn, and Dorcas moved slowly to the house, her thoughts bouncing from one person to another.

The kitchen was empty at the moment, but that wouldn't last long. She hung up a damp dish towel and wiped the counter automatically.

Her little sister with two babies… It was hard to believe. At least Grace wasn't too far away. With a driver, they could be there in less than two hours. She tried not to wish them back in Lost Creek. Ezra would be taking over the farm from his father when the time was right, and it had made sense for them to settle there.

Still, at a time like this Grace would want her people around her, the way Dorcas had. She had an irrational sadness at the thought of Grace's twins growing up without their aunts and uncles and cousins surrounding them.

She stood for a moment, her hands

clasped on the edge of the sink. If Katie's mother had stayed here, they wouldn't now be faced with such difficult decisions.

We're trying hard, Mary Ann. Trying to do the right thing for your precious Katie.

What would Jacob have said to her if they hadn't been interrupted by the phone call? He'd held her hands in his, and at the thought she felt them again, felt them enclosing hers in a warm, strong grip. And saw again the look in his eyes…a look she hadn't be able to turn away from.

A warm flood of emotion poured through her, and she knew in that moment what it was. She loved him. She loved Jacob Unger, and there wasn't a chance of that leading to anything but sorrow for her.

Chapter Nine

Dorcas awoke early the next day after a disturbed night. A glance at the window revealed nothing but gray mist—fog had enveloped the valley. It seemed to press against the windows, making the idea of subsiding on her pillow and pulling up the quilt very attractive.

But the children were stirring already, and she'd long ago decided that the best policy was to be awake when they were. Otherwise, the day tended to get out of hand.

When Luke was alive it was different,

of course. Every once in a while, he'd stoop over her side of the bed, tuck the covers over her and whisper that he'd deal with the young ones. How she'd treasured that extra hour of sleep.

Not today, though. She slipped out of bed, washed and dressed quickly. Even so, she heard Sarry and Katie in the kitchen and smiled at their chatter. Sarry didn't warm up to just anyone, but she'd taken to Katie as if they'd spent their lives together.

Jacob was another person she'd taken to, but Dorcas had already decided firmly that Jacob had to stay out of her thoughts. No one must know what she felt, because everyone already knew that he was still tied to his last wife.

Putting a smile on her face, she joined Sarry and Katie in the kitchen.

Katie swung away from the stove as Dorcas appeared. "Look, Cousin Dorcas.

These were on the back porch when we came down."

Several boxes sat against the wall, and she knew immediately what they were. A quick look confirmed it…boxes of diapers, several pairs of onesies and a baby quilt.

"Word got around like lightning, ain't so? The next person to go to Lancaster County will have a car filled with packages."

Sarry nodded, flipping scrambled eggs into a bowl. "There will be more," she said.

Sure enough, by afternoon the pile was taking up so much space that they began carrying it into the sewing room. Dorcas stood back, frowning a little. "I suppose we should repack all of this so that it'll be easier to take."

"Not right now," Katie said and then flushed when Dorcas stared at her. "I just meant you look so tired. It doesn't have to be done now. You could take a nap."

She should have realized Katie would see that something was wrong. She was very quick at figuring out people. Except for her uncle, of course.

Dorcas shook her head. "Ach, I can never sleep during the day. I'm fine."

"Are you wishing you were there with your sister?" Something seemed to strike Katie. "If I weren't here, maybe you could have gone. I'm sorry."

"Ach, don't be so foolish. That's not it at all." Dorcas smiled, shaking her head. "I'd love to be there, but it was more important for Mammi, and we couldn't both be gone."

Katie stared down at another package of diapers. "When my mammi was sick..." She pressed her lips closed.

It was clear what she was thinking, and

Dorcas reached out to touch her shoulder, then turned her gently so she could see her face.

"When your mammi was sick, I wanted to be with her. But it wasn't long after Luke died, and Matty was just a baby. Sometimes you want to be in two places at once, but Mammi always says, 'Do the thing in front of you.'"

Sarry joined in on the last few words they'd heard so often, and then added, "Mammi says that's probably the thing God wants."

For a moment the three of them stood together, and Dorcas had to blink back tears. How fortunate she was, and how God had blessed her. He'd blessed her with kinder and family to love and now He'd brought Katie into her life.

And Katie had brought Jacob. Even though Dorcas felt the pain of loss when she thought of Jacob, she couldn't feel regret. Without knowing it, he had taught her that she could love again. Surely that was a blessing, wasn't it?

Jacob told himself that he was glad to be back in his own house again. He dropped his suitcase by the door. The living room was peaceful, he decided. Not a speck of dust on anything, and not a single thing out of place.

He'd make coffee and grab some bread and cheese before going over to the machine shop. The kitchen was equally neat and clean. Quiet.

Well, that was how he liked it. No sense in comparing it to Dorcas's place, filled with the thuds and shouts that made three young boys sound like thirty or the laughter and chatter of women. Or even James's house, echoing of crying babies and toddlers' squeals. He liked his quiet, peaceful house.

Lifeless, something in the back of his mind shouted. *Lifeless, that's what it is.*

Impatient with himself, he cut into a loaf of stale bread and lopped off a chunk of cheese. It was certain sure time he'd come home. This was the life he'd been given. He'd made up his mind about that when he'd found his wife gone and a note on the kitchen table. He was a success at business and a failure with people.

Still, there had been moments in the past few weeks when he'd caught a glimpse of another life, another person… a person who had family, friends, people who counted on him. A person he wasn't sure he could be.

Shaking his head, he poured out a mug of coffee and carried it with him the short distance to the shop.

When he entered the office, he found

Reuben on the phone that was an essential part of business.

"Here he is now." He held out the phone, smiling a welcome. "Call for you from James Miller over in Lost Creek."

Instantly visualizing an accident involving Katie or one of the others, he snatched the phone. "What is it? What's wrong?"

James's chuckle made the tension seep out of things. "Sorry, sorry. Didn't mean to scare you. I tried to reach you before you left, but you were already gone."

"Yah, I needed an early start." He nodded at Reuben, who was heading for the door. "What's happening?"

Once he was alone, he settled at his desk to hear what James had to say.

"Everyone's okay, first. But I just heard yesterday that the owners of the old lamp factory in Fisherdale finally decided to sell the property. Seems like it might be what you're looking for, so I wanted to let you know."

"Denke." His thoughts tumbled faster than he could find words, and he made encouraging noises while James described the cement block building and surrounding property.

Fisherdale. It wasn't more than twelve miles from Lost Creek. At least he was somewhat familiar with the area, and thanks to Katie, he now knew some people there who might ease the way to acceptance. But did he really want to start his new branch there?

It would certainly mean spending more time there, at least until the place was up and running. More time with Katie, and that meant more time with Dorcas and her family.

His thoughts settled on an image…an image of Dorcas's hands in his, of looking deep into her eyes and not being able to pull his gaze away.

"So, what do you think?" James's voice broke through his thoughts.

"It does sound possible." He didn't know what he wanted. The wisest thing to do was surely to stay away from Dorcas as much as he could...wisest for both of them.

"If you're interested, I can get hold of the seller and arrange a time for you to see it."

James sounded delighted at the idea of helping him. That wasn't surprising. James's cheerful, open face formed in front of him. James was as generous and helpful as his sister.

His mind started working again. "I need to be here a few days at least. Suppose I call you back early next week."

"Yah, sure, that's fine." James's enthusiasm sounded dampened, but that couldn't be helped.

"Later, then. Denke, James." He hung up quickly. It was a mistake to mix business with friendship. A person ran too much risk of hurting someone.

The truth was that not only did he need to be here for the sake of the business, he needed to stay away from Lost Creek and Dorcas until he was sure what he ought to be doing.

Dorcas's kitchen was filled with the aroma of roast chicken, rhubarb pie and a sense of anticipation. At least, it felt that way to Dorcas. She hadn't realized how much she'd been missing Mammi and Daad until she knew he, at least, was on his way.

James and his family were already here, with Anna helping Sarry with the vegetables while Katie held the baby.

The boys had taken the toddlers out to play in the yard. Dorcas looked out now and then, hoping they weren't being too rough with the little ones. She could remember a few mishaps when Matty was that age and trying to keep up with his brothers.

At least Timothy was much more mature now than he had been then. He was giving the younger one a piggyback ride, while Silas rolled a ball back and forth and Matty chased it when it went out of their circle.

Smiling, she went back to making the gravy thickening. They were good young ones, all of them. Daad would be so pleased to see them that the conversation she wanted, no, needed to have with him would have to wait.

What had Lizzie told Mamm and Daad about Katie Unger? And about her uncle? She'd assured herself that Mamm and

Daad knew Aunt Lizzie well enough to take it all with a grain of salt. Now that the moment was upon them, she found her assurance slipping away and her nerves jangling.

The door opened and Daad was there, surrounded by all the young ones who'd been outside, all talking at once. Dorcas grabbed a towel to wipe her hands and rushed to get her chance at a hug.

"Dorcas," he murmured, and she felt the reassuring grasp of his strong arms around her. Daad had always felt like a rock to her, and she didn't want to let go.

But she had to, of course. The others were waiting for their turn. Daad's hands cradled her face, and he looked into her eyes for a moment, seeming to smile at what he saw there before he was swept away by Sarry.

It wasn't until much later that a chance came for a private talk, when James and

Anna had gone and Sarry and Katie were putting the boys to bed.

She sank down in her rocking chair, looking at her father in the high-backed chair that had been Luke's favorite. "It's gut to have you home, Daad. We missed you."

He nodded, looking very relaxed. "I'd been doing nothing much for too long. It's fine for your mamm… There are always things for her to do. But once I'd held those healthy little boys, I knew there wasn't anything more to do there. And I'd left the farm for too long at this time of year. Not that James didn't do a fine job," he added quickly, making her laugh.

"I know he did. But you just want to see for yourself that planting is going well, ain't so?"

"Yah, that's it. And it is, thanks to James." He hesitated. "And young Katie is a sweet girl. Think of her being Mary Ann's daughter. She has a look of Mary Ann, yah?"

"She's like her mother, I think." She relaxed a little more. Daad could see what a sweet child she was. "So what did Aunt Lizzie tell you?"

He looked as if he'd deny hearing from Lizzie, but then he chuckled. "Ach, you know how Lizzie is. Seeing trouble everywhere she looks. I've often wondered why."

Dorcas shrugged. "Maybe she can't help it."

"Your mamm felt bad for you, having to deal with Lizzie. But Mammi and I knew you'd be all right."

"I wish I'd had your confidence," she murmured. "I just hated to think that rumors would spoil Katie's visit, but it didn't seem to. Maybe teenagers don't pay attention to what Lizzie says."

Daad was studying her face, and she knew he was waiting for her to bring up Jacob Unger. Somehow she couldn't find the right words. Anything she said might make it sound as if he was too important.

"So, tell me a bit about this Jacob Unger. Mary Ann's brother-in-law, yah?"

Daad had gotten tired of waiting for her, Dorcas guessed.

"I should think you'd heard enough about him from James," she said, sounding a bit exasperated. James had spent most of the meal talking about his call to Jacob and the chance of his opening a branch of his business close by.

"But I didn't hear what you think, daughter," he said gently. "You've seen quite a bit of him, ain't so?"

She felt humbled by his tone. "Sorry," she murmured. "Yah, I have seen him, mostly because of Katie." She frowned, trying to find the right way to tell it.

"When he first came here trying to find Katie, I thought he was some sort of an ogre from what Katie said."

"And he wasn't?"

Dorcas shook her head. "Just mostly an ordinary man without much experience with children. Especially teenage girls."

Laughter rippled through her at the thought of Jacob and Katie shouting at each other with Katie on the porch roof.

"Katie would be a challenge for anyone. She's as spirited as Mary Ann was, and I keep remembering some of the things she got up to."

"Yah, she was," Daad agreed. "But a dear child all the same."

"I finally realized that here was one last thing I could do for Mary Ann. Try to make peace between them and help them find the right path to the future." She shook her head, thinking she may as well be honest about it. "It's not easy."

"No, it wouldn't be." He paused, studying her face, and reached out to clasp her hands. "Lizzie seems to think you are infatuated with him. That was the word she used," he added quickly, as if to deny it was his thought.

"I was afraid of that. Well, she's wrong, that's all." Infatuated was certain sure not the word for what she was.

He patted the hands he held. "I trust you, daughter. If you like him, that's enough for me."

"Denke," she said softly, feeling tears spring to her eyes at his faith in her.

"If you need help, you'll tell me." He sounded sure of it. "And now I'd best go home and let you get some sleep."

He rose, but before he reached the door, he turned. "Mammi and I love you, child."

He went out, leaving her comforted.

Chapter Ten

The fact that her father was back made Dorcas aware of how stressed she had been without Daad to fall back on. Of course, she'd always known she could call him with any problem, but it wasn't the same. In fact, this was the first time in years that Daad and Mamm had both been away for any length of time.

After a cold, rainy day yesterday, today was sunny and warm. When she went outside, she saw that the tulips were close to blossoming and stopped to admire them. The rain seemed to have brought everything along, and the haze of green on the trees announced that winter was over.

The boys were off school this afternoon because of a meeting for the Amish teachers in the district, but Sarry had taken Timothy and Matty over to see Anna, and Katie had gone to town with Becky and Betsy. Sally had promised she wouldn't let anyone buy anything foolish.

And Silas—where was he? She'd seen him going off toward the woods. But here he came now, scurrying along the path in some excitement.

"Silas? Is something wrong?"

He was shaking his head and out of breath when he reached her, but he wore a big smile.

"Violets," he exclaimed. "Lots of violets down by the stream. And I think a jack-in-the-pulpit. Come and see!"

He grabbed her hand, tugging at her. She held back for an instant, thinking of all she had to do. But how often did she do something with Silas, her quiet one, always such a thinker. Smiling, she half walked, half ran with him back to the path that led to the creek. Out of breath, she slackened to a walk, laughing at herself.

"Slow down. They'll still be there in a few more minutes."

Silas smiled, his eyes sparkling. "But I get to show you first, before anyone else."

Her heart tumbled over. With the three boys so close in age, did the middle one get less than his share of attention?

"That is special. For me, too." Dorcas suddenly felt as if they were in harmony with each other and the peaceful woods and burbling stream.

Parenting had been easier when Luke

was here. He often said that being a father was the most important thing he'd ever do, and he put his heart into it. How she had loved watching him wrestling and tumbling with the boys, always so gentle, and all of them laughing.

"Here," Silas announced when they reached the creek. "Just look. Isn't it pretty?"

Dorcas responded with a long, indrawn breath. The sheltered place on the bank was covered with the delicate purple blossoms, so lush she wanted to bury her face in them. "The best they've ever looked, I think. So thick and pretty."

The violets always seemed to like this sheltered spot near the stream. And she did, too. It was her favorite place on the farm.

"Look at this." Silas scrambled over one of the large, smooth rocks. "Is this a jack-in-the-pulpit?"

She climbed over and knelt next to him, loving the excitement on his face. "Yah, for sure. Look, here are the two leaves coming up. And here, in between them, is the stem that will have the flower. In another few days or a week, it will be out." She sighed with satisfaction. "I think spring is my favorite season."

He giggled, looking suddenly as if he was about five. "When we went out to collect the colored leaves, you said that fall was your favorite season."

She grabbed his straw hat and tilted it down over his eyes. "You caught me. I guess they're all my favorites. Wouldn't it be boring to live where seasons didn't change?"

He nodded vigorously. "I'll always live right here," he announced. "It's where I belong."

Tired of kneeling on the stones, she got

up, rubbed her knees and took the long step over to the large, flat rock where the stream made a little pond. She sat down, pleased the rock was warm. A person couldn't really count on it this time of year.

Silas followed, squirming down beside her, then leaned over, attracted by a flicker of movement in the silvery water. "Minnows," he said with satisfaction. "Tiny baby minnows."

She nodded, feeling relaxed and satisfied. "This is a special spot. Did you know that your daadi asked me to marry him right here?"

Silas's eyes grew wide. "He did? You know what? He taught me how to make a little boat with a leaf for a sail right here. Maybe this was his favorite place, too."

"I think you're right."

Silas wiggled around so that he was sitting closer to her. He seemed so receptive that she put her arm around him. Sometimes when she did that he slid away, but today he leaned against her. She looked down on the back of his neck as he snuggled against her, thinking how fragile it looked in spite of how he was growing.

"When Daadi asked you, were you very happy?" He didn't look up as he asked the question, instead staring at the sandy bottom of the creek.

"For sure. I loved him very much. We were very happy together." She wasn't sure where he was going with this, but she suspected he wanted to say something important. At least, important to him.

"Do you think you might marry someone else sometime?" He murmured the question so softly she almost missed it.

It was a good thing Dorcas was sitting down or she might have fallen. "What made you think of that?" Dorcas needed time for a careful answer.

But she didn't get the time she wanted. Instead he just shrugged and looked up at her, his eyes deep blue and serious, needing an answer.

"I'm not sure, Silas. But if I did, I'd have to be sure it was right for everyone, not just me." She prayed it was the right thing to say. "We'd all talk about it to decide. Okay?"

He nodded, seeming satisfied, and she thought he was reassured and finished with the subject. But it seemed she was wrong, because he started again.

"We were talking about it—I mean, Katie was talking to Sarry," he added. "Katie said it might be a gut idea if you married her onkel Jacob. Then Katie and Jacob could both stay here. Is that okay?" He glanced at her quickly, as if afraid she might be annoyed.

She took a deep breath, praying again that the good Lord would give her the best answer. He'd trusted her with these precious lives, so she had to trust He would guide her words.

"It's okay for anybody to think about it, yah. But maybe not so good to talk to people outside the family. That would be gossip, ain't so?"

He nodded, looking very solemn. She felt pretty solemn herself. This had been the last thing she'd expected to hear from her quiet one, but she knew he was a deep thinker.

If Katie and her boys were wishing for that, she was afraid they were going to be disappointed. It seemed to her that Jacob's farewell had been close to being final.

As Dorcas emerged from the woods, she spotted Sally's buggy turning in at her lane. Good, that meant Katie was back. Maybe she could get some help getting the rest of the laundry off the line before it was time to make supper.

Still shaken a little over Silas's confidences, she walked across the lawn toward them as Sally stopped at the hitching rail. Katie, all smiles, was chatting away as she climbed down, carrying a large bundle of something.

"It's sensible, I promise," Sally commented, waving at her.

"But is Katie?" she asked.

Sally's lips twitched. "Not bad." She turned away to shake her head at her daughters, who were apparently excited because Katie had asked them to stay for supper.

"No," she said firmly to all three of them. "Sometime when Dorcas knows about it ahead of time. You don't make plans unless your hostess knows about it. You should know that."

"Soon," Dorcas said, nodding to the twins as Sally turned her buggy. "Denke, Sally. This was so nice of you."

Katie echoed her thanks, clutching her package with one arm and waving good-bye with the other as they drove away.

"Careful." Dorcas put a protective hand under the slipping bundle.

Katie grasped it. "Come inside so I can show you." Her face was alive with excitement. "I can't wait for you to see what I got."

Judging by the look of it, Katie had gotten some fabric, apparently planning to make something. Once they were inside, she dropped it on the table and opened it. "There," she said. "Isn't it pretty? Sally helped me pick it."

"Sally has a good eye for color, working so much with quilts." Washing her hands quickly, Dorcas came back to touch the fabric—a smooth, light cotton in a delicate shade of peach. "Ach, that's beautiful." Close on that thought came another. "I hope you had enough money with you."

Katie nodded. "Yah, I was fine." She held the fabric up near her face. "Sally said this is a good way to tell if the color's right for you."

She smiled, remembering Sally doing just that on long-ago fabric shopping trips. "Yah—"

She stopped, put off by the sound of feet on the back porch. Matty and Timothy rushed in, followed closely by Sarry.

"What did you get?" Matty lunged toward the table, hand outstretched. Katie shrieked and pulled her fabric away.

"Dirt!" she exclaimed.

Dorcas wondered why she'd ever thought that girls were quieter than boys. She caught Matty's hands before he could try again, reflecting that boys were certainly dirtier.

"You know better than to come in the kitchen with dirty hands. Out, both of you."

Sarry eyed them with satisfaction. "I told you." She came closer to have a look at the material herself. "So pretty."

"Can we start it right away?" Katie was practically bouncing with excitement.

It was a shame to douse her pleasure, but Dorcas had to shake her head. "Afraid not now. I have to bring some clothes in from the line before I start supper, and there's not enough time. Maybe after supper."

Katie's face fell. "Please. I could do it."

Dorcas reminded herself that she'd just been thinking how fortunate a person she was. Naturally, she'd have troubles. Everyone did.

"Cutting is a challenge, and once you cut into the material, you can't undo it. And we'll have to find a pattern to fit you. After supper, not now."

Katie pouted, but she said no more, carrying her fabric into the sewing room. When she returned, her sparkle was back, and she carried a laundry basket.

"I'll help you," she said, and they went out to the yard together.

Up and down, Dorcas thought. She seemed to remember that from her teenage years. At least Katie recovered quickly.

The wind had picked up, and it had the sheets fluttering and whipping around. After several efforts at one especially obstinate one, Katie collapsed in laughter.

Dorcas chuckled, invigorated by the

wind whipping past her. “No sheet is going to get away from us.” She grabbed it. “Can you get that other end?”

Katie made a jump and came down with the edge of the sheet. They started to fold, coming forward and backward as they brought end to end. Katie, she realized, still had that excited look in her eyes, as if she anticipated something special coming her way. The new dress, she supposed.

“I’m doing pretty well with driving the pony cart, ain’t so?” Katie asked the question out of the blue, making Dorcas a bit cautious in her answer.

“I haven’t ridden with you lately, but Sarry seemed happy with you.”

“I like riding with Sarry. She doesn’t tell me so much about it as Timothy does.” Katie wrinkled her nose. “I don’t need to know everything.”

"Timothy probably thinks he should explain as he goes," Dorcas said.

"Yah. He wants to impress Onkel Jacob." Katie said the words as if it was common knowledge.

Dorcas blinked. First Silas, now Katie. How was it that everyone seemed to know more about what was happening than she did?

By Monday, Jacob had found a number of reasons why he needed to go back to Lost Creek. He wasn't sure how valid they were, but they'd seemed good enough that here he was, sitting next to Charlie Downs, heading back.

He told himself he owed it to James at least to look at the place he'd found for him. That didn't mean it had anything to do with Dorcas.

Charlie was taking him straight to the building in Fisherdale, and they were in good time to meet the owner, Max Jackson. Jacob hadn't actually talked with the man. His contact had been with Jackson's daughter, Eileen, who'd seemed pleasant enough.

He glanced toward Charlie. Charlie had looked just a little amused when he'd told him, making him wonder if there was something more about Jackson that he should know.

"According to James's directions, the property should be coming up somewhere after the next bend." He leaned forward in an effort to spot it.

"No worries. I know the place. It's only a few miles from Lost Creek and right on the edge of Fisherdale. Been sitting empty for a good long time."

"I hope it's suitable. I've looked at enough wrecks to make me wonder."

Charlie nodded. "I hope so, too. The building looks pretty messy from the outside. Still, it shouldn't be bad to fix up." He slowed the car. "Be nice to have another Amish business in the area."

They'd cleared the curve in the road, and Charlie pulled off onto a gravel lot, dotted with places where the weeds had broken through. He stopped in front of a large, cement-block building and shut off the ignition.

"Glad Max decided to sell the building." Charlie peered through the windshield. "I don't like to see a place deteriorate. There's no sense in that. Waste, I call it."

It was easy to see why Charlie got along with his Amish friends and customers—they shared an attitude that said usefulness was important, both in people and in objects.

"Yah, I know what you mean," he murmured, scanning the building while he spoke. It reminded him somewhat of a typical fire hall with its square, boxy shape and the large bay door on one side. Make it easy to bring things in and out, he'd say.

"It was used as a storage space for quite a few years, mostly for old Max's auction business. He did that after he closed the lamp factory." He chuckled. "He was quite a character. You should have heard him running an auction back when he was in his prime. He'd have people laughing and bidding and not even noticing they were paying more than they'd intended."

"Auction fever," Jacob said. "My daad used to say that you had to take someone with you to say no once in a while."

He hadn't thought of that in years, and it made him smile. Daad started taking him to auctions when he was a kid. Those were great times.

Brushing the memories away for the moment, he opened the door. "Think I'll walk around the outside since they're not here yet. You interested?"

Truthfully, he'd like to hear Charlie's comments. This was his territory, after all.

Charlie joined him, and they started walking around the building. A few broken windows along the back, probably kids monkeying around. It didn't look as if they'd gone inside.

Charlie shook his head at the sight. "Those broken windows probably date from last year. Max should have had them fixed."

"What are you doing here, Charlie Downs? Don't you have enough to do at work?" The voice was loud, but the man was small, shrunken and wrinkled, Jacob saw when they turned around.

"This is my job now, Max. You're out of date. I'm driving folks around these days. This here's Jacob Unger. He came over from Bellport to have a look at this old place."

A hearty laugh shook the man's frame, followed by a coughing spell. A woman Jacob guessed was the daughter he'd talked to came hurrying up.

"There, you see?" She handed her father a tissue. "I keep telling you don't do things that make you cough."

"Don't do this, don't do that." He waved away the tissues. "Anybody would think you wanted to keep me around."

"So I do. I'm sure I don't know why." Her plump figure shook with laughter, and she turned to the two men, smiling. "Charlie, nice to see you." She zeroed in on Jacob. "You'd be Mr. Unger. Glad you came by. It's past time we got rid of this place."

Her father jostled her with an elbow. "What are you trying to do—run the price down?" When he smiled their faces were oddly alike, even though hers was pink and plump and his was as wrinkled as old leather.

"Eileen, you open the doors and let them look around. I'm going to sit a bit." Leaving them to it, he dragged up a metal barrel, turned it upright and sat.

Jacob exchanged looks with Charlie, and they went on inside. "It's connected to the electric, right?" Charlie said, glancing at the woman.

She nodded. "It's turned off now, of course. And maybe you wouldn't want it, anyway, being Amish and all. What was it you said you wanted it for?"

"A machine shop." He didn't bother to explain the sorts of things they made and repaired, figuring she wouldn't be interested. Even now, she was turning toward the door.

"I'll go keep an eye on my dad. Take your time. There's no rush." She walked out briskly, the bright pink skirt she wore ruffling around her knees.

Jacob found Charlie an invaluable aid. He knew the history of the building, and he had a sharp eye for possible problems. He was the one who spotted the place where the roof had leaked.

They made a good job of it, and once they finished, Jacob had to admit that it was a good match for what he wanted. Better than anything else he'd seen.

But did he want his new branch here? That was what it came down to. It was a bit farther than he'd pictured, but the building was more suitable than anything else he'd seen. And from what Charlie said, the jobs would be welcome.

And then there was the other matter. Did he really want the shop to be this close to Dorcas and her family? Not that he'd have to spend much time here. He could put Reuben in charge here and stay in Bellport where he was settled.

A few minutes later, he was explaining to Max Jackson that he needed some time to think about it, maybe bring his manager to have a look, too.

Jackson shrugged, looking tired. "Take your time, but I'm not holding it for anyone. The first person to put money in my hand will get it."

Charlie started the car, waiting while the others pulled out, and then looked at Jacob. "Where to?"

He opened his mouth to say that Charlie could drop him at the inn. Instead he heard himself saying Charlie could drop him at the farm. "I should talk to James about it. Since he suggested it, I mean."

Charlie nodded, but his lips twitched a bit, as if thinking there might be another reason. "You want me to drop your bags at the inn? It's not out of my way."

"That would be a help. I spoke to Molly Esch on the phone so she's expecting me," he said, referring to the young Amish woman who ran the place for the elderly woman who owned it.

"I'll do that. Just let me know when you need me." He glanced ahead as they rounded the bend, and the car's movement jolted a little.

Jacob saw what Charlie had seen a moment later. A shiny red pickup stood blocking the lane to Dorcas's place, and a teenage boy leaned out of the window, talking to the girl who stood laughing and talking. It was Katie—Katie whose laughter checked at the sight of Charlie's car. She backed away a few steps, and in the next moment the pickup roared off down the road.

"You want to pick her up?" Charlie said when he didn't speak.

"Yah." He opened the window as the

car drew up beside Katie. "Get in," he snapped and closed his lips firmly. He wouldn't air his anger in front of Charlie.

He didn't know who to blame for this—Katie or that boy. But he'd certain sure find out.

Chapter Eleven

Dorcas was cleaning a pailful of strawberries when she heard a vehicle pull up outside. She moved to the window to see Charlie's car. Jacob was back, as James had been predicting, sitting in the front next to Charlie.

But before Jacob moved, Katie jumped out of the back seat. She ran into the house, passed Dorcas without looking, thudded up the steps and slammed the door to her bedroom.

Dorcas stood there, staring after her in surprise for a moment. Then Jacob followed Katie inside and the expression on his face cleared up the situation. Obviously Katie had done something her uncle found inappropriate. *Again*, she added silently.

Jacob's jaw was clenched, and his eyes were dark with disappointment. "I have to talk to her," he said, barely looking at her.

"Maybe you should calm down a little first," she ventured without much hope.

Jacob's gaze settled on her, and that look chilled her. It was as if they were right back at the beginning again—as if all the talks and the feelings that had passed between them hadn't existed.

Dorcas turned away, not wanting him to see her face. Her heart sank. All this time she'd done her best, and it wasn't good enough. They were right back at the beginning again.

"Katie went upstairs to her room." She

gestured, remembering how she'd kept him from going upstairs that first day. She just didn't have the strength to keep doing things that didn't work. "The third room on the left."

He headed for the steps, and Dorcas busied herself with setting out snacks for the boys. They'd be home from school soon. She would think about that to stop herself from dwelling on things that would hurt. Still, despite her best intentions, she couldn't help but listen to the sound of footsteps upstairs, of a door opening.

Thank goodness the boys came thundering in just then, making it impossible to hear anything else. Even as she greeted them cheerfully and started pouring lemonade, she realized they knew something was wrong. The younger boys seemed to shake it off, but Timothy looked toward the stairs apprehensively until Dorcas touched his shoulder lightly.

"School all right today?"

He nodded, but he still watched the stairs.

"We talked about the last day of school picnic," Matty said, bouncing on his chair. "You're going to help, ain't so?"

"Mammi always helps," Silas said. He sounded as if that was as established rule. Actually, she supposed it was. The mothers always helped for the picnic, so of course she would.

"Do you know what I should bring yet?" She'd rather talk about picnic food than what was going on upstairs.

"Whoopie pies," Matty declared. "You make the best whoopie pies. Better than anybody."

"Maybe. But how about some snickerdoodles for now?" She set the plate of still warm snickerdoodles on the table.

"Yum." Silas grabbed a handful before Matty could dive in. As for Timothy…he still looked toward the stairs. It had even distracted him from snickerdoodles.

Now what? she wondered. He almost looked guilty, but how could he be? Whatever Katie had done, he wasn't involved.

The screen door clattered, and Sarry came in with a basket of eggs. She glanced toward the sound of voices upstairs and then shrugged. "Lemonade," she murmured.

Dorcas nodded, pouring a few more glasses. Whatever happened, the lemonade wouldn't go to waste.

When they heard footsteps on the stairs a few minutes later, all five of them were sitting around the table snacking. Katie came straight to Dorcas.

"I'm sorry, Cousin Dorcas." Her voice trembled just a little, but then it steadied. "I didn't mean to upset you."

Then she turned to glare at her uncle. "Only I don't see that I did anything wrong." This last came out in a defiant declaration.

Dorcas rejected the impulse to lock Katie and Jacob both in a room together until they figured out how to get along. But before she could come up with anything else, Katie was bursting out again.

"I don't see what's wrong with saying hello to an Englischer who was driving past. He wasn't a stranger."

"No, I didn't think he was." Jacob sounded as if that might have been preferable.

Katie held her head high, frowning at her uncle. "I saw him when we went to the fabric store. What was wrong with that?"

Jacob scowled. "What was a teenage Englischer doing in a fabric store?"

Katie looked likely to say something to fan the flames, but Sarry got in first.

"Patches," she declared.

Jacob looked stunned for a moment. Then he shook his head. "Patches?"

Dorcas decided it was her turn. "Those rounds of fabric that the kids wear on their jackets. They carry them at the fabric store with different things embroidered on them."

Jacob looked harassed, as he often did when she took a hand in his discussions with Katie. "What does that have to do with it?"

"You asked," she said, shrugging. "Sally took Katie and her two girls shopping for fabric."

He rubbed the back of his neck. "It doesn't matter what they went for. I don't want..." He stopped, seeming to notice that all of them were staring at him. "We'll talk about this later."

She wasn't sure whether he meant her or Katie, but either way, later was better. Maybe it was time to take herself out of the situation completely. She'd tried, again and again both for Mary Ann's sake and for Katie's, but she seemed to fail every time.

Katie and Jacob weren't any closer to getting along together, and the only person who was hurt was herself.

She stood up, her palms flat on the table. "If that's all, you kids had best be off to your chores."

"But Mammi..." Matty began and let the words die away. "Can we take a cookie with us?" he coaxed.

Dorcas's smile broke through. "Yah, you can. Just don't feed them to the chickens. Or the goat."

The boys scrambled out the door, cookies in hand. Jacob stood staring out the window. After exchanging looks, Sarry and Katie went out.

The kitchen was extremely quiet when they'd all gone. Jacob glanced at her, then shook his head and looked away.

"I need to see James. Do you know where he is?"

Feeling deflated, she shook her head. "Either at his place or over at Daad's, getting the milking shed ready."

Jacob nodded shortly and headed for the door. When he reached it, he paused for a moment. "I'm sorry," he said and walked out.

Sorry? She sank back into her chair. Sorry for what? For turning her life upside down? For showing her what it might be like to love again? Or for going away without a proper conversation?

Jacob stood for a moment on the lane, trying to unscramble his thoughts. Too much had been happening too fast, and he suspected he hadn't handled any of it very well.

One thing at a time. He needed to talk to James. He had gone to some trouble to line up this visit to Max Jackson's property, for which he must be thanked. All of Dorcas's family had extended themselves to be helpful, and he hadn't done much to show his appreciation. Even Katie, with her tantrums, had done a better job than he had.

He rubbed the back of his neck, trying to release the tension there, and he started walking toward the lane. He'd cross the road to James's place, and if he wasn't there, he'd obviously be getting ready to help with the milking. Once he'd thanked James properly, maybe he'd be in better shape to figure out what to do next.

Anna was in the yard taking down baby

laundry. At his question, she pointed him toward the path that ran between the fields, ending at the dairy farm. Nodding, he cut across that way.

James was in the milking shed, doing some of the endless cleaning that went with dairy farming. There was an older man with him, and it didn't take much imagination to realize they were father and son. Abel Miller was what James would be in another twenty years or so… stocky, broad shouldered, with blue eyes that crinkled with laughter.

"You'd be Jacob Unger, ain't so? Wilkom. I've been hearing a lot about you." He didn't say whether what he'd heard was good or bad, but at least he was smiling.

"Your family's been wonderful helpful to me and my niece. I'm grateful."

Those blue eyes seemed to look right through him, much the way his daad's always had. He hoped they didn't pick up all the mistakes he'd been making with his niece.

"Mary Ann's daughter is part of our family, too. I hear you're finding a teen-age girl a challenge." His lips twitched, and something in Jacob relaxed.

"That's certain sure. I think I'd take a dozen boys rather than a teenage girl." That was probably the first time he'd been able to joke about it, and that seemed freeing.

"The only way to cope with one is to have her from babyhood," Abel declared, "and to have a good wife to help you."

That might have stung, but Jacob knew it was only a statement of fact.

Abel was already turning away from them. "I'll leave you two by yourselves. You'll want to be talking about how you made out with Max Jackson."

"You don't need to..." Jacob began,

but he'd already headed out of the milking shed.

"What did you think of old Max?" James was saying as he picked up the hose. Automatically Jacob grabbed a long-handled brush and began sluicing the water around.

"He's a character, all right." Jacob frowned, thinking over that conversation. "I couldn't tell whether he really wanted to get rid of the place or not. Or how long he'd wait for me to make up my mind."

"Yah, he's always been one to hold on to what he has," James agreed. "From what I heard, his health hasn't been good, and his daughter would like to be rid of that place. But would it be suitable for what you have in mind?"

Jacob stared at the stream of water for a moment, picturing the place in his mind. "It would need some fixing up, but it would make a decent machine shop with enough space for some bigger things we deal with." He hesitated. "A lot depends on the people around here… whether the bishop would have any objections, whether there are some experienced men around as well as the kind of young men we'd want to take on for apprentices."

"You'd be best off talking to the bishop yourself about that, but as far as Jackson is concerned, well, Dorcas knows the family better than I do."

"Dorcas?" That startled him. Dorcas hadn't mentioned a thing about it. Come to think of it, she probably hadn't had time.

James was nodding. "They used to live in Lost Creek, and she did cleaning for them for a time after his wife died."

"I didn't realize. Yah, I should talk to her about it, and see what my manager has to say. He might want to come and have a look."

It felt strange to refer to Reuben that way, but that was exactly what Reuben had become. Why had it taken so long for him to realize how capable Reuben was?

Maybe his troubles with Katie hadn't been entirely unfortunate. He'd begun to see things in a different way since he'd been forced to accept help. Still, he'd be glad to get back to his familiar surroundings.

It had been in the back of Jacob's mind that Reuben would take over the new place while he continued to handle the existing business. But would Reuben want that? A talk with him was long overdue.

"Don't look so discouraged." James clapped him on the shoulder. "It will work out."

He nodded, wishing he felt that sure. It seemed the deeper he went into this situation, the more difficult it became.

He tried to respond with a smile. "I'd best get busy, then. Denke, James. I appreciate all your help."

By the time he crossed the road again, Dorcas filled his thoughts. The one person who'd been the most help to him, and he still hadn't thought to ask her advice. How ungrateful he must seem for all she'd done for Katie. And for him.

If only… His train of thought came to a sudden halt. The bushes beside the road rustled, and Timothy emerged and fell into step with him. It looked like the boy had been waiting for him.

"Timothy?" He made the name a question, seeing the concern that seemed to weigh on the boy. "Was ist letz? What's wrong?"

"I thought… I wanted…" He stumbled,

tried to speak and then let the words slip away. Obviously something was wrong.

He hesitated a moment before putting a hand on Timothy's shoulder. When Timothy didn't pull away, Jacob moved them both to the side of the lane. They could lean against the split rail fence and talk where no one would notice them. If Timothy would talk. Right now he stared steadily at the ground in front of him.

"Komm," Jacob said gently, feeling the tension that kept Timothy's shoulder rigid under his hand. If he couldn't even get a ten-year-old to talk to him, what good was he? "Tell me about it."

Timothy was still for another moment. Then he nodded, still studying the ground. "I… I came down here before." He waved his hand toward the mailbox. "Mammi asked me to get the mail."

"Right." That, it seemed, was the easy part. "And then?"

"That pickup truck—it pulled up there." He gestured toward the place on the verge where the vehicle had been. "You know, the red one. The one you saw." His voice trembled.

Jacob nodded, smoothing his hand on Timothy's shoulder. "Go on."

Timothy swallowed hard. "He started to talk. Seemed friendly, and told me about the truck. It was new, he said."

"I guess he was proud of it." Jacob could guess what was coming. Even Amish boys were interested in motor vehicles.

The boy nodded. "He talked a little bit, and then he asked me if Katie lived here." He shot a quick glance toward Jacob's face and away again. "Only I don't think he knew her name, because he just said the pretty girl with yellow hair."

"And you told him yes." Jacob might

wish for an instant that Timothy had said no, but he couldn't really feel that.

"Then he handed me a dollar." Timothy's eyes grew wide, making Jacob wonder if he'd ever had one of his own. "He said it was mine if I'd go and tell her he was here. I… I didn't think it was wrong, but then there was so much trouble." He sniffled, rubbing his nose with his sleeve. "And you blamed Katie, but it was really my fault, too. Please don't be mad at Katie." He watched for Jacob's reaction with an anguished expression.

Had he implied that boys were easier to raise than girls? Well, he'd been wrong. Poor Timothy was struggling to know what was right, and he'd reached out to Jacob, who had plenty of struggles of his own. Still, there was no doubt in his mind of what he had to say.

"Ach, Timothy, it wasn't your fault." He patted the boy's shoulder, drawing him closer. "You answered his question truthfully. Nobody will blame you for that."

It had been Katie who'd decided to respond.

Timothy was shaking his head even before he finished. "Maybe, but I knew something was wrong when he offered me the dollar." He held out a damp, wrinkled bill, looking eager to be rid of it. "I don't want it."

He didn't, either, Jacob thought, but saying that wouldn't make Timothy feel better. "Suppose we put it in the jar Mammi has for people in need. Then it will do some good. Okay?"

Timothy's expression cleared. "Yah. Denke." He hesitated and then looked up into Jacob's face. "Now will you be friends with Katie again?"

"Yah, I will. I promise." Jacob felt moved in a way he hadn't in a very long time. He'd be friends with Katie again, for Timothy's sake. And if he could, he'd be friends with Dorcas again, too.

Leaving the chicken casserole baking in the oven, Dorcas stepped out onto the porch, wondering where everyone had gone. A gaze around showed her two figures coming up the lane together—Jacob and Timothy. They seemed to be deep in conversation, and her Timothy was looking up at Jacob with such a serious expression that she felt a pang in her heart. Timothy was her child, not his. If Timothy had any secrets to confide, he should be talking to her, not to Jacob.

Was she jealous? Dorcas turned away, staring intently at the garden instead of the two of them. She and Timothy had always been so close, especially since Luke passed.

She shook off the thought, trying to

be fair. If Timothy had found relief in talking to Jacob, she shouldn't complain. After all, she encouraged Katie to talk to her.

She'd still like to know what they were talking about, but she wouldn't stand here and stare at them. Grabbing the basket she kept on the porch, Dorcas moved quickly to the garden, bending to pick some leaf lettuce for supper. The first row was almost gone, but there was a later row coming along.

Halfway down the row, Dorcas felt her breathing grow slower and her muscles relax. How could she…could anyone… come into a garden and not feel at peace?

Her thoughts slipped to prayer without even planning it. Since Luke had passed, she'd taken problems, even small ones, to the Lord, and she'd always come away comforted.

She wasn't sure how long had passed

before Sarry came up and took the basket from her. "I rinse, yah?"

"Yah, Sarry. Denke." Dorcas gave her sister a quick hug, carried back in time to the moment when Daadi put the small, blanket-wrapped bundle in her five-year-old arms. "You are such a blessing to me."

Sarry blushed, as she always did when she didn't know what to say. Then she planted a kiss on Dorcas's cheek and trotted toward the kitchen with the basket.

Jacob stood outside the phone shanty, and Timothy must have gone to do his chores. After a moment's hesitation, she walked over toward him. She wouldn't bring up his conversation with Timothy, of course. But if it came up… And she still hadn't heard what he thought of that old building of Max Jackson's.

Jacob's smile was tentative at first,

but it widened when he realized that she looked friendly. He gestured toward the phone shanty as she joined him.

"I hope it's okay to make some calls. I want to talk to Reuben about the building I saw today." He paused. "According to James, you know the Jackson family."

She nodded. "I used to, anyway." James must have told him that she used to work for them. "They're a nice family, for all that Max is a little crochety. His bark is worse than his bite, I know that."

"I got some mixed feelings about whether he really wanted to sell or not. And then he turned around and pushed me for a quick decision."

"Was his daughter there with him?" she asked.

"Yah. She took him away before we had a chance to go into details."

"I'm sure she'll talk some sense into him. She's the only one left in the area, and the responsibility rests on her. If you're patient..."

Jacob's lips twitched. "You're thinking I'm not good at that, yah?"

"Well..." She found herself relaxing.

"I'll try," he promised. He glanced back at the phone, as if thinking about the decisions to be made.

"What does Reuben think about the building? And what do you think, as well? I haven't seen it in a long time, but gossip is that it's falling to bits."

"Not quite that bad, but it will need some money spent on it if we decide we want it."

Her lips twitched a little as she noticed that he said "we" now. There was a time when he'd made all the decisions on his own.

"Now you're laughing at me." He leaned against the shanty. "That's better than having you angry at me." His eyes grew very serious all of a sudden.

"I… I wasn't angry," she stammered. "I was just…"

"Discouraged," he filled in for her. "I was, as well. Each time I vow that I won't lose my temper with Katie, and then something sets me off. But I realized something this time."

She looked up, wondering what was on his mind.

His expression grew serious. "I see now that it affects other people, too. The kinder, you…" He touched her fingers with the lightest of touches, and that touch seemed to shimmer across her skin. "I am sorry. I know you've heard it before, but this time…"

"When it comes to children, especially teenagers, you have to go through it over and over again," she said quickly. "Don't give up."

Maybe it was a reminder to her not to give up on Jacob and Katie, as well.

Jacob nodded, studying her face as if reading her thoughts. “Your father said something like that to me earlier.”

“He did? But where did you meet him?” She hadn’t expected it, but she should have. “What did he say?”

Jacob seemed to be focused on something beyond her, but he answered. “Your daad said that to raise teenage girls, you needed to know them from the time they were born, and you needed to have a good wife to help you.”

The words struck her like a blow as she saw what that would mean to him. “I’m so sorry. Daad wouldn’t have known about your wife. He’d never have said it otherwise. I hope you won’t hold it against him.” Her hand closed over his in sympathetic understanding.

“Ach, don’t be foolish. I understood.”

He patted her hand gently and stood looking down at their clasped hands for a long moment.

Then he spoke very softly, so that she had to strain to make out the words.

"Teresa wouldn't have been that, even if she hadn't died."

Dorcas gasped, thinking she must have misunderstood. But he was already turning away, striding off toward the barn. He probably thought she hadn't heard. She wished she hadn't.

Chapter Twelve

Looking for Katie alone to make friends with her, as he'd promised Timothy, Jacob struggled to keep his mind on what he was going to say to her. He wanted her to realize the potential danger of going off that way, but just how did he do that and not get her mad at him again?

Scouring his mind for a solution didn't seem to be helping. Maybe he'd do better to trust inspiration on the spur of the moment.

He forced his attention back to the long conversation he'd had with Reuben. But even the press of business hadn't been enough to wipe out of his mind his unguarded reaction to Dorcas, when she'd tried to sympathize with his supposed grief and pain over Teresa. He'd been living a lie for such a long time. Why now had the truth spurted to the surface in that way?

Dorcas hadn't heard him, he told himself. She hadn't said anything, so she'd probably missed it entirely. And even if she had caught something, she couldn't know what it meant.

He rounded the corner of the barn and came upon Katie, bending over the fence near that pesky pet goat of Silas's. She held out a palmful of grain that the goat gobbled enthusiastically.

"Better not give him too much, or he'll jump right out of his pen," he said, walking over to her.

Katie was the one who jumped. He'd

startled her. It took her a moment to put on her offended look, obviously wanting him to know she was still annoyed with him—her head up, her eyes narrowed and her teeth clenched.

He nearly laughed, but managed to restrain it. She wouldn't understand, but in that moment Katie looked so much like her father. Phillip had just that look, like an angry cat, when he was annoyed.

Funny. Usually Katie looked so much like Mary Ann, with her quicksilver changes of mood and her sparkling eyes, but now… He thought of his younger brother and seemed to feel the gaping hole where his brother's love and dependence had been.

"Is that all you want?" Katie must have gotten tired of waiting for him to say something else. She left her hand out too long, though, and the goat nipped at it.

"Ouch!" She yanked it away, shaking it.

"Did it break the skin?" He grasped it so he could see, but there was only a small pink imprint of the goat's front teeth, already fading.

"It's nothing," she snapped, yanking her hand back and rubbing it.

Reminding himself that she was all that was left of his little brother, he managed a smile and a soft reply. "Ach, Katie, let's not fight. I'm sorry I came on so strong."

"Well, then, why did you? It was embarrassing, being yanked into the car like that, and then letting everyone see you were mad at me."

"I was mad, yah, but mostly I was scared. Couldn't you see that?"

Her eyes widened, and she stared at him. "Scared? You're never scared of anything."

He couldn't help chuckling at that. "Sure I am. I'm scared of lightning storms and that mischievous goat...and of losing you or letting you get hurt."

Katie's face softened. "I'm not hurt."

"No, you're not, thank the gut Lord. But when I saw you standing all alone by that strange truck, I panicked. All I could think of was to get you safe."

And that was the truth of it, although he hadn't intended to say all that. Behind his anger was absolute terror that something bad would happen to her and it would be his fault. For an instant the thought of Teresa stabbed at his heart, and he couldn't get that door closed fast enough.

"I... I never thought of that." Katie actually seemed to be considering his words. "Dorcas..."

He was quick to pick up the hint. "Dorcas loves you, too. She would be just as hurt if there was a chance of anything happening to you."

"But nothing did." Her voice went up just a little.

"Not this time." He had sense enough to leave it at that.

He could feel her eyes on him, could feel the moment when her gaze became speculative. What was she planning now? He didn't doubt there was something.

She changed the subject abruptly, maybe knowing there was no point in continuing the quarrel. "I saw you were talking to Reuben. Are you going back home again soon?"

Shrugging, he started back toward the house, and she walked with him. "In a day or two. I need to talk things over with Reuben and make some plans."

"But you'll be back, won't you? You'll be back by Saturday."

"I haven't really thought about it. Does it matter?" He wanted to set up a time when Reuben could look at the building so he could have Reuben's help in firming up an offer.

"Saturday's the Mud Sale." Katie looked as if she couldn't believe he'd forgotten it, and he didn't think he'd ever known anything about it.

"There's nothing I need at the moment. If you want to buy something…"

Katie shook her head violently. "We… me and the boys…we thought you'd be here to help. Dorcas is going to have a stand, and we're all helping. You have to come or you'll spoil everything."

He started to ask how on earth he could spoil anything by not being there for a Mud Sale, but what difference did it make? He and Reuben would want to come over the weekend, anyway, when the shop was closed.

"Yah, all right. I'll be there to help. Okay?"

Katie's look of relief made him apprehensive. What on earth were she and the boys planning?

Dorcas shook her head over the pair of little boy pants she was patching. Or rather, trying to patch. She'd begun to think it was hopeless.

As she started to throw it back into the sewing basket, a hand interrupted her. She looked up, startled to find Aunt Lizzie settling into the rocking chair next to her on the back porch.

"Here, I'll do those for you while we talk." She picked up the needle and thread Dorcas had been using.

"You surprised me, Aunt Lizzie." Surprised was probably the best word. It wasn't necessarily a good surprise. She'd figure that out once she knew what was on Aunt Lizzie's mind.

"I was over at your brother's, so I thought I'd drop in on you before I head back to your cousin Lida's place."

She held up the pair of pants, revealing the hole that had taken up much of the seat. "Gracious, what did the boy do with these pants—use them to carry a load of coal?"

Dorcas had to laugh. Aunt Lizzie was in a good mood, it seemed. Otherwise, that criticism of the pants would have been sharper, including raising her children to think their clothes grew on trees.

"It looks like it, doesn't it?" Dorcas picked up a shirt with a seam that was splitting. "This pair of pants had survived Timothy and Silas, but Matty seems to have meant the end of it. Just toss it in the basket, and I'll use it for cleaning rags."

"Nonsense." Aunt Lizzie began searching through the basket for a patch. "Always something you can do to get another wearing out of them. My, you should see how Anna's baby is growing out of his nightgowns. I told her I'd make up a couple more for him. I have some of that blue flannel left."

"That's wonderful gut of you. I'm sure Anna appreciates it. She doesn't have much time to sew."

That explained the good mood. Aunt Lizzie had been visiting with the little ones. She made no secret of the fact that she preferred babies to children.

"Anna said that Jacob Unger is around again. I suppose that means you still have Katie."

She decided to choose her words carefully. "Katie is still visiting. Her uncle is traveling a lot right now, setting up a new machine shop. She's too young to be alone, and we're happy to have her."

Aunt Lizzie sniffed. "He's finding a way to make even more money, I suppose. My second cousin Selma Schmidt lives over there in Bellport, and she says he's what they call an Amish millionaire."

Dorcas tried to get her mouth open in time to deny wanting to hear what Aunt Lizzie's second cousin thought, but since she had several pins in her lips, that didn't work. It should teach her a lesson. Mammi was always trying to break her of that habit.

She removed the pins and pushed them into the pin cushion. "I don't think there are any such things," she said.

"Oh, don't you believe that. They say Unger makes money hand over fist with those parts he makes for Englisch companies. Using computers." She snorted.

"Whoever heard of Amish businesses using computers?"

Dorcas suspected that Aunt Lizzie knew more than one computer user. She just didn't know about it. They weren't uncommon in some Amish businesses.

Aunt Lizzie took quick, even stitches as she fitted the patch into place. While admiring the needlework, Dorcas doubted she'd ever get Matty to wear them, but she held her tongue.

"Not only that, but they say he's going to start one of his factories or whatever he calls them right around here. We'll see what the bishop says about that."

Once again she held her tongue, but she was covertly looking around to see where Jacob was. Maybe back in the phone shanty, or out at the barn with the boys? He wouldn't leave without saying goodbye, would he?

"Dorcas, are you listening to me?"

Aunt Lizzie's sharp voice brought her back to the moment.

"Something about the Mud Sale? Sorry, I was wondering whether Silas might have outgrown this shirt."

At least, she had been, hadn't she?

"I asked what you're doing at the Mud Sale on Saturday. With three of your kinder in the school, you certain sure ought to be contributing to the fundraising."

"Yah, of course." She wasn't sure why Aunt Lizzie made a person feel guilty even when the answer was yes. "I volunteered to run the candy apples stand." She went on with another question before Aunt Lizzie could interrupt. "Do you think we should have caramel apples, too? The committee was talking about it, and—"

"Not unless they've got more help than I think they do. You couldn't be making two different kinds, and that hot caramel is too dangerous to have around your kinder. Why didn't you volunteer to do the popcorn, or something simpler?"

"Well, as you said, with three scholars in the school, I feel as if I should be doing one of the more difficult jobs, don't you think?"

She glanced at Aunt Lizzie to see how she was taking that, only to find she wasn't paying any attention at all. She was staring toward the phone shanty, and Dorcas had a sinking feeling she knew why.

Jacob stood there looking at her and hesitating, almost as if he knew about Aunt Lizzie. Probably the children had been talking.

"What is that man doing here?" Aunt Lizzie whispered the words, probably not wanting to draw his attention, but Dorcas didn't think it was working.

"He stopped by to see his niece while he was in this area. Isn't that just what you'd expect him to do?" she added.

"He's coming over here." Aunt Lizzie shot to her feet, dropping the sewing she'd had on her lap. "Dorcas, I'm very disappointed in you. It's not for lack of warning. I told you myself—"

She cut off short as Jacob approached, gave a curt nod in his direction and fled back through the house the way she'd come.

"Was that the Aunt Lizzie I've heard about?" Jacob put one foot on the porch step and leaned forward, so that he was at eye level with her.

"It's the only Aunt Lizzie we have, so it must be, yah? What did you hear?"

"That she's cranky, that she's a blabbermaul, that she doesn't like children, or teenagers, or… Shall I go on?"

Dorcas dropped the sewing in her lap.

"I can see I'll have to talk to the boys about gossiping themselves. I thought they knew better."

He gave a rueful chuckle. "I'm afraid I encouraged them to talk." His expression sobered. "I didn't realize that my being here was causing so much trouble for you."

The caring in his look made her heart turn over. "Ach, it's not a problem. In any event, it's my own decision." She smiled and shook her head. "Dealing with Aunt Lizzie is almost a weekly event, and it's good for developing patience. I can use some lessons in that."

"Not as much as I could."

He meant with Katie, of course. "Have you talked with Katie?"

"Cautiously," he said, but he seemed to be laughing at himself. He hesitated, and she wondered if he'd say more. Finally he went on.

"The only thing I could find to tell her was how I felt when I saw her standing there alone with a stranger in a truck."

"Terrified?" she asked.

"That's about it." His hands, linked lightly on his knee, tightened all in a moment. "All the bad things you read about in the newspaper flooded through my mind at once. I guess you know."

Dorcas closed her eyes for a second, trying to block out the possibilities of what might happen to a child alone. "Yah, I know. It's hard to…well, to find a balance between keeping them safe and giving them responsibility."

"That's for sure." His words were so heartfelt that Dorcas had to smile.

"Being a parent is like that," she said.

"I guess I never thought of myself as Katie's parent until she jolted me into it by running away. That was a wake-up call for sure."

"It's better now?" The lilt in her voice was meant to encourage him, and she thought it succeeded.

"Yah. We forgave each other. We're friends again, as Timothy says."

She thought instantly of the two of them walking up the lane together. "I saw you talking with him." She left it open, not asking what her son had confided, but hoping.

Jacob smiled, but he shook his head slightly. "You wouldn't want me to break a confidence, would you?"

"I guess not." Her tone was rueful.

He patted her hand and then let his rest on hers. His warmth was reassuring. He wouldn't let her child down.

"About the Jackson property..." he said with a glance at the phone shanty. "It looks like I'll have to go back to Bellport tomorrow."

"Already?" She hoped that didn't sound as disappointed as she felt.

"I'm afraid so." He looked as if he was trying to decide how much to say, and in the end decided on very little. "I've got to work with Reuben on some information before making up my mind. But I'll be back on Saturday, don't worry."

She stared at him in puzzlement. "Why would I worry? I mean, we'll be glad to see you whenever you come."

"According to the children, it's important to be here for the Mud Sale."

While she puzzled over that, his hand slid away from hers slowly. Reluctantly? She wasn't sure. He straightened.

"Denke, Dorcas. I'm grateful for your help. Always."

Chapter Thirteen

The rest of the week went by slowly, and Dorcas found it hard to convince herself that Jacob's absence had nothing to do with it. She had been happy and content before she met him, and she'd be happy and content once he'd disappeared from her life for good.

Strangely enough, that didn't seem to raise her spirits, and when the week culminated in what looked like being an all-day rain on Friday, she wondered if the week would ever end.

It was a relief to gaze through the

window and see the boys emerge from the path that led to the school. Seeing her watching, they waved and darted through the downpour to thump their way up the three steps to the back porch.

As Dorcas turned away from the window, the back door burst open and Matty plunged in, wet, muddy boots and all. "Matty, stop!" she shouted.

He stopped, teetering almost as if he'd tumble out of his boots. "Why?"

"Look at your boots and tell me why." Dorcas started toward him, but Sarry reached him first. She picked him up and shifted him back outside the door.

"Yuck!" she said with emphasis, pointing to the clumps of mud clinging to his boots.

"Oh!" He bent over, staring. "I forgot."

Balancing like a tightrope walker, he stood on one foot struggling with the boot until Silas, exasperated because he was blocking the way into the kitchen, grabbed it and yanked it off. Matty stumbled backward into Timothy, who banged against the door.

Dorcas found a sharp word on the tip of the tongue and yanked it back. What was wrong with her? Shaking her head, she hustled them all inside, making sure the boots were lined up on the rubber mat outside.

"Snack time," she announced. They scrambled to the table, where Sarry and Katie were already setting out glasses of milk and a plate of cookies.

With a smile of thanks, she turned back to the basket of apples on the counter. Tomorrow they'd be busy with the Mud Sale stand whether it was raining or not. She glanced at the boys, thinking what a mess they'd make of themselves in the field around the fire hall if it rained. They'd probably enjoy it all the more, though they'd start by complaining.

As if on cue, Matty gulped down the last of his milk, put his glass in the sink and went to the window, pressing his face against the water-stained glass.

"Isn't it *ever* going to stop raining?"

Katie, coming up behind him and ruffling his hair, shook her head. "Maybe it will rain for forty days and forty nights, like in the Bible."

He swung around, looking up at her with a dismayed face. "It won't, will it? I want to go to the Mud Sale tomorrow and have popcorn and candy apple and cotton candy..."

Katie squeezed him, laughing. "If you have all that, you'll be too sick to worry about the rain. Anyway, I think it will stop tonight."

"And tomorrow there'll be lots of mud," Silas added.

"That's why it's called a mud sale," Silas and Timothy said together, making them all laugh.

The kitchen seemed warm and cozy with the rain drumming on the roof and the love inside. She found herself looking at Katie and thinking how much they'd miss her when Jacob took her away.

Sarry, who often seemed to guess what she was thinking, came to help her dump apples into the large washing pan. "Katie should stay." The words, in her soft, slurred speech, touched Dorcas's heart.

"I wish she could," she echoed.

But it wasn't going to happen. Sooner or later, Jacob would find a housekeeper to live in his house and look after Katie, and before long he'd also make a decision about his new machine shop. Then they'd both be settled back in Bellport. She was going to miss them, and so would everyone else.

The sound of raised voices broke into her musing, and she found Timothy and Matty confronting each other. "He said he'd come!" Matty almost shouted the words.

Timothy, looking sorry he'd provoked his little brother, was quick to hush him. "Okay, okay. I didn't say he wouldn't come. I just said maybe with the rain and all, he might change his plans."

Jacob, obviously.

"He won't. He promised." Matty's little face set in stubborn lines. "He has to be, or—"

Katie and Timothy exchanged looks and burst into speech almost simultaneously. "It'll be okay." Timothy drowned her out. "Don't worry."

"He'll come," Katie declared, "because it's business." She said the words as if they were the deciding factor.

Dorcas discovered she didn't want

to leave it at that, even though it might be true.

"Jacob promised he'd come for the Mud Sale, so he'll come," she said flatly. "Now, if you'll get your rain gear on again and do your chores, we'll have plenty of time to work on the first batch of candy apples." She held up an apple in each hand. "You want to help, don't you?"

There was a rush toward the door. Giggling at the sight, Katie went to help them, and in a few minutes the kitchen was quiet again.

Dorcas glanced at the tubful of apples. Aunt Lizzie, despite her grumbling, was right about one thing. The candy syrup was dangerous around children. But she wouldn't deprive them of the joy of contributing. No matter how many other things went wrong or how many sorrows you had, there was always joy in helping others.

* * *

Asking Charlie to drop their bags at the inn, Jacob and Reuben finally got to the Mud Sale in the late afternoon on Saturday.

Reuben lingered at the side of the road for a moment. "It certain sure is a Mud Sale."

"At least the rain stopped in time."

Jacob let his gaze wander over the gravel lane leading up to the fire hall. There was a gravel area probably meant for parking, but today it was filled with stands of all sorts. A makeshift stage stood in the middle, surrounded by folding chairs filled with folks ready to bid on the items the auctioneer was hawking.

He started down the lane. "Let's see if we can find Katie or any of the Miller family. There should be a candied apple stand somewhere here."

Jacob spotted Timothy on the far side of the auction area, but before he could call out, Timothy had squirmed through the crowd in the other direction. Then he popped up again, this time with Katie, pointing them out to her.

"There's Katie." He returned her wave and started toward her, then realized that Reuben had stopped to look at some double and single harrows set out in the grass.

"You want to shop?" he asked, hesitating.

Reuben shrugged. "Maybe. I wouldn't mind looking. I could use one of those single harrows, if it would fit in Charlie's trunk."

"Okay, you do that. I'll catch up with you later."

Reuben was already measuring the harrow he had his eye on, and Jacob smiled and shook his head. He should have remembered that Reuben was a bargain hunter. No doubt he wouldn't leave here without buying something, even if it wasn't the harrow.

Striding off toward Katie, he gave her a quick hug. "Gut to see you. Where's everyone else?"

For some reason, Katie seemed distracted, glancing around as if searching for someone. He thought briefly on that Englischer and dismissed the idea. She couldn't hope to meet up with him at a place like this.

"Everyone is getting something to eat. Komm, I'll take you to Dorcas at the stand. We'll all meet up there."

"Is Dorcas by herself? Why aren't you helping?" He followed her, dodging through the crowd, and bit his tongue. He'd been determined not to start off criticizing, and it was the first thing he did.

Fortunately Katie didn't seem to notice, or if she did, it didn't bother her. She sidestepped around a courting couple that seemed determined to stay linked together and skirted a pair of young girls waving mammoth cones of cotton candy. He dodged the cotton candy and followed her. The combined scents of cotton candy, funnel cakes, donuts, fudge, apple dumplings and finally candy apples had his mouth watering.

But he was more interested in the woman behind the counter, serving up a couple of shiny dark red apples on sticks. Dorcas looked up and saw him, and a smile lit her face. He doubled his pace and nearly avoided contact with one of the sticky apples.

"Dorcas." He said her name and then found he was standing there looking at her and thinking he'd missed her.

"You made it. Wilkom. Would you like

a candy apple?" She held one out, but he shook his head.

"Maybe later. Why don't you have any help?"

"Why don't you go in and help her?" Katie said, sassy and smiling. "I'm supposed to go and make sure the boys eat something other than sweets."

That struck him as a good idea, and he lifted the flap in the counter that allowed him to get inside next to Dorcas. "You do that, then." He put a twenty in her hand. "Your treat."

"You don't need..." Dorcas began, but he shook his head.

"It's a good cause, ain't so?"

She nodded, her lips curving again. "Very good. We need a new roof put on the schoolhouse this year."

"You made all of these?" He glanced at the array of apples on trays, ready for dipping. Another tray held those that were finished and ready for sale.

"With Sarry and Katie's help. And some input from the boys, too. We did a big batch last night, so we'd have them to start out with. Want to try your hand?"

She picked up one of the uncoated apples and held it out to him.

He shook his head. "Only after you demonstrate," he said teasingly. "You wouldn't want me to get injured, would you?"

"The trick is to keep your fingers well away from the sugar syrup if you don't want a nasty burn." She dunked the apple into the syrup, twirled it until it was completely covered, and lifted it onto a tray covered in wax paper. "Now you."

Standing close behind her, he held another apple hovering over the bubbling syrup. "Maybe you'd better help me."

"I never thought I'd hear you say that." Her face, inches from his, crinkled with laughter. Then she closed her hand over his, and they swirled the apple together.

"Onkel Jacob!" Katie's shout startled him so much that his hand nearly hit the hot syrup.

"Katie," he began, but she was already reaching out for Dorcas.

"We can't find Matty. We've looked everywhere, and we don't know where he is. You have to come." She lifted the counter, tugging Dorcas out. "The boys and Sarry are looking at that end, so I said you and Onkel Jacob would look from here out to the road. I can take care of the stand."

"Wait a minute." Jacob's natural inclination was not to let anyone rush him. "Where have you looked? Have you asked people at the stands?"

"Never mind that." Katie yanked at

him. "If he sees you and his mother, he'll come."

He opened his mouth to argue, but a glance at Dorcas's white face silenced him. He caught hold of her hand, and they cut quickly across the gravel toward the next stand.

Dorcas felt her thoughts spinning out of control as they scurried around the sausage stand. Jacob explained quickly to the Englisch stall holder, and the owner and his daughter turned away from their counter to search inside.

"Do you want one of us to help?" The young woman gave Dorcas a look full of sympathy. "My dad can manage..."

Dorcas blinked back tears at the woman's kindness. "Denke...thanks, but if he's just hiding..."

"Sure, I remember doing the same thing as a kid. I wouldn't have come out for a stranger." She patted Dorcas's arm. "Just let us know if we can help."

"She's right, you know." Jacob's voice was deep with reassurance. "That's probably the answer. Just a silly prank on his brothers."

She took a breath, trying to settle her jangled nerves. "I should have asked Katie or Sarry to watch out for him."

"He was with the whole group..." Jacob began.

"Yah. When everyone is watching, then nobody is." That probably didn't make sense to him, but it did to her. "If he is just hiding..." She stopped where she was, turning to scan the area out toward the road, shaking when a car went flying past.

Jacob gripped her hand tightly. "Stop thinking he'd go out there. He couldn't hide anyplace out there, and there'd be no reason for it."

"You think there has to be a reason?" For a moment her temper flared. Unjustly, of course. He was trying to help.

"Matty seems like a pretty sensible little guy," he said, his tone quiet. Patient. "He knows he's not allowed out on the road. I don't think he'd go out there without a good reason."

"Yah, you're right." Her voice trembled a little. "It was just not knowing where he is." And fearing she'd let him down.

Jacob held both her hands in his for a moment, not speaking, and she felt his strength flowing into her. "Komm. Let's work our way back toward the others. Maybe they've found him by now."

Predictably, Jacob searched methodically, not letting her race off looking futilely here and there. He kept her from running, but he couldn't still the racing of her pulse or the guilt that battered her.

They'd reached the rows of chairs when Jacob stopped. "Here, let's ask the auctioneer to call for him. That might bring him out."

Not waiting for a response, he led her toward the platform. Young Adam Esch, helping with the auction, came over when Jacob beckoned, and in a moment the speaker boomed loudly.

"Matthew Bitler. Your mammi is waiting for you by the auction stage. Komm on up here now. Matthew Bitler…" He started again, and the buzz from the crowd silenced. Everyone seemed to be waiting, listening, looking around.

A long moment, then another. Then someone shouted, and she realized it was Timothy. "Here he is."

Timothy, pulling his little brother behind him, emerged from the back of the quilt display. They headed for her, and the crowd reacted with a wave of laughter and clapping.

Matty broke free of Timothy's hold and ran straight into Dorcas's arms. She held his little body tight against hers, feeling his damp breath against her cheek.

"I'm sorry, Mammi. I fell asleep."

Laughing a little, she brushed his silky hair back out of his eyes. "So long as you're all right."

Timothy had reached them by then, and Matty started apologizing again. "I'm sorry, Timothy. I didn't mean to fall asleep. I wasn't supposed to."

Timothy gave his brother a hasty nudge. "Silly. For sure you shouldn't have." Timothy glanced up at Dorcas, then shifted to Jacob. "Sorry," he muttered.

Jacob looked as if a lecture hovered on his tongue, and she shook her head slightly. Something seemed not quite right, but this wasn't the place to delve into it.

"Back to the stand now, everybody. Komm." As Dorcas shooed them toward the candy apple stand, Silas and Sarry came around the back of the auction stand to join them.

"Everyone is looking at us," Jacob muttered as he fell into step with Dorcas.

Dorcas gave him a sympathetic look, knowing he didn't feel at home here. "At least most of them are looking friendly. Except for the ones who are saying, 'What kind of mother lets her six-year-old wander off?'"

That seemed to chase away his embarrassment. "They aren't. Or if they are, it's because they don't remember what six-year-olds are like."

She blinked, surprised at his insight.

Before she could comment on it, she caught a look on Sarry's face that made her look again. Sarry was staring at the ground, her lower lip pushed forward in its most stubborn expression.

"Sarry? Is there something I should know about?"

Sarry shook her head, and her gaze refused to meet Dorcas's.

Dorcas knew the signs. Sarry was aware of something that had her torn between doing one thing or another. Her answer to that was always to settle on stubborn silence, and there was no point in pushing. That would just make her more unhappy.

They reached the stand to find both Daad and James there already, wanting to scoop up Matty and tease him about getting his name announced on the speaker. She sighed, exasperated. If they didn't stop, they'd make him think he'd done something wonderful instead of something naughty.

"Enough of that," a voice proclaimed, and Dorcas realized that Aunt Lizzie, of all people, was inside the stand with Katie. "Matthew was a naughty boy to scare everyone that way. Ain't so, Dorcas?"

She didn't want to agree with Aunt Lizzie's hectoring tone, but she'd said just what Dorcas was thinking, so she had no choice.

"Aunt Lizzie is right. No more hiding, Matty. You'd best stay right where I can see you."

Matty opened his mouth to argue, then thought the better of it. He nodded, but she noticed the resentful look he sent toward Timothy. Yah, something was going on that she should know about. This wasn't the time or the place, but eventually she'd find out.

"Candy apples for everyone," Daad said, gesturing to Katie. She smiled, looking relieved, and began setting out the candy apples.

"Not for me," Aunt Lizzie declared. "My stomach is too old for candy apples, and so is yours, Abel. You'd be better off with some nice applesauce."

Naturally that made Daad insist that he could eat a dozen candy apples without ill effects, and with a good deal of laughing and teasing, the moment passed.

Dorcas glanced at Jacob to share a laugh, but he was looking thoughtfully at Katie, then at the boys.

She leaned toward him and spoke softly. "I know. Something's going on, but this isn't the place."

He nodded, and Dorcas felt a bond of agreement and understanding between them. She enjoyed it for a moment, and then she reminded herself that Jacob's business would soon be finished. He'd go home then, and he wouldn't be coming back.

Chapter Fourteen

Jacob was relieved when the Mud Sale finally came to its conclusion. People were packing up, closing down stalls, loading prized purchases into cars. Reuben had not, after all, bought a harrow, but had found a few smaller items he could carry easily.

At Jacob's suggestion, Reuben had walked back to the inn while he stayed to help Dorcas and her family pack up. That would be his chance to find out if there really had been something planned about Matty's disappearance.

He'd told himself several times that it was a foolish idea. Matty wouldn't want to upset his mammi, would he? On the other hand, a six-year-old might not realize how upsetting his disappearance would be.

He couldn't get out of his head that remark Matty had made…something about not being supposed to fall asleep. Why would he say that unless something was set up about the whole thing?

Timothy would know, if that was the case, and he was tempted to talk to the boy. But Dorcas might well resent his taking it upon himself to interfere with her discipline.

No, his only course was to talk to Katie. She'd been with the kinder most of the day. If they'd been planning a trick or a joke, she'd know about it.

When he reached the stand, he found that Abel and James were already dismantling the stand. He reached up to hold the crosspiece that Abel was working on, and together they took down the canvas side. Apparently the stands were dismantled between one event and another and stored in a shed on the property.

Together they folded the canvas and then went on to the next.

"How did everything go with the building you're considering? Did you come to terms with Max?"

"Not yet." Naturally James would be interested. "We discussed price, but we'll have to estimate the cost we'd have to spend on getting it in order. It is the best possibility we've seen for what we want, though."

"Gut," he said heartily. "We'll hope it works out. We could use another Amish business right here in Lost Creek. No one wants to see our young folks have to travel far to get a job."

Jacob nodded in agreement. If he had a son, he'd certain sure not want to see him working someplace away from home.

"We should be able to make an offer soon. I ought to talk to the bishop, to find out what he'd think about it. Not everyone is comfortable with a stranger coming in."

"Ach, you're not a stranger." Abel's face split in a grin. "We've seen plenty of you and Katie. As far as the bishop is concerned, if you and your friend want to go to worship with us tomorrow, you'd have a chance to talk to the bishop and some of the other men afterward. They're eager to hear all about it."

So word was spreading through the community. He wasn't surprised, but he hoped people weren't going to be disappointed. It wasn't a done deal yet.

Nothing he could do but agree, though. "That'll be fine. It's good of you." He caught sight of Katie, putting a bushel of unused apples in the buggy. "I need to talk to Katie about something," he said quickly. "I'll be back to help soon."

Jacob saw the moment when Katie spotted him coming. She abruptly veered in the other direction. No, she wasn't getting away from him that easily. He lengthened his stride and caught up with her before she could slip into the fire hall.

"Hold it." He drew her away from the door. "You may as well put that basket down, because we're going to have a talk."

Katie gave him her most innocent look. "But I… I'm supposed to put these in the buggy."

"Then you're going the wrong direction, aren't you? Come on, Katie. What was the idea of telling us that story about

Matty being lost? You knew all along that he wasn't lost, didn't you?"

"I don't know what you mean," she declared, but her eyes avoided his.

He ignored that protest. It was clear from her efforts to scoot away from him that she knew exactly what he meant. He took a firm grip on his temper.

"You may as well spill the story. If you don't, it'll be easy enough to get it out of Matty. He all but gave it away already."

"We should have known." Katie's eyes snapped. "It's no good expecting Matty to keep a secret. Everything he thinks comes right out of his mouth."

"Why?" The edge of his annoyance showed. "It was a mean thing to do to Dorcas. How could you?"

"I didn't realize," she wailed, dissolving suddenly. "I didn't think she'd get that upset."

"You should have. Where was your

common sense?" He had an urge to shake her.

Somebody grabbed his arm. "Don't. Don't blame Katie." Timothy's face was almost as white as his mother's had been. "It wasn't just Katie. We all talked about it." He stared at the ground, unable to meet Jacob's eyes. "We thought it was a gut idea."

"A good idea!" He would explode soon. Dorcas might be cut out to deal with this, but he certain sure wasn't. "Why? Just tell me why?"

It was Katie's turn to grab his arm and deflect his attention. "We just thought it would be nice if you and Cousin Dorcas had some time together." Again the innocent look appeared. "You said yourself that you never got a complete conversation without one of us interrupting."

"Yah," Timothy said eagerly. "We thought you'd go looking for Matty together. That's all. It would be nice for you to be together."

Jacob opened his mouth, but the words got lost on the way out. He saw what this was all about. He should have realized sooner. They were playing matchmaker. Thoughts rushed through his head… James and Sarry welcoming him with open arms… Abel going out of his way to smooth the path with the bishop…

They thought he was courting Dorcas. Most likely the whole Amish community thought that by now. Even Charlie had been hinting, and he hadn't seen it.

Worse, Dorcas probably thought so, too. How could he have been so blind?

The attraction he felt for her was real, but marriage? He'd never thought he'd marry again. He'd been convinced it was impossible. How could he, with the secret he'd been carrying all these years?

It would take an extraordinary woman to deal with that secret. Not that Dorcas wasn't extraordinary, but there was her family, too. What could he say?

He looked at the two young ones staring at him, expecting him to know what to do. And he didn't. He didn't.

Dorcas carried another tray of desserts out to the table after worship the next day. Another sunny, warm May day greeted her, and she paused, raising her face to the kiss of sunshine. Yesterday had been so busy and upsetting that she really needed the peace of Sabbath. They all did, she supposed.

Setting the tray down, she helped herself to a piece of chocolate cake with peanut butter frosting and took a look around to be sure all her family was accounted for before relaxing. Sarry was keeping an eye on the boys playing kickball. Katie, holding Anna's youngest, was helping to watch the babies and toddlers.

As for Daad and James…that was predictable. They were part of a group clustered around the bishop, asking Jacob and Reuben questions about their business.

Dorcas let her gaze linger on Jacob's face for a moment. She'd been trying to keep her mind off him since yesterday's foolishness, but just now he was fully occupied by the discussion, and it was safe to look without being seen.

How was he coping with the children's matchmaking efforts? He had known what was going on even before she did. Why hadn't he told her himself? He'd let her find out from Timothy.

Timothy and Katie had been sorrier

than she could have imagined. At least that was to their credit. They hadn't realized the effect their prank would have on her. They couldn't know that it touched the most vulnerable part of her—the part that feared she couldn't keep the children safe without Luke.

She pressed her palm against her heart. It was an actual physical pain, as if someone had stuck a knife in. She'd never realized, until it happened, what the words a broken heart meant.

A rustling beside her announced the arrival of her friend Sally, carrying two mugs of coffee.

"You share the cake, and I'll share the coffee," she said.

Dorcas passed her a paper plate containing a piece of the angel food cake she loved. "There you are." She lifted the mug and held it between her palms, the warmth comforting her.

"Have you and Jacob talked about what the kinder were doing yesterday?" Sally always figured out the things that affected her.

Dorcas grimaced. "He seems to be avoiding the whole thing. I think he hadn't even begun to guess what they were thinking."

"But you knew," Sally said.

"Not to say knew," she corrected. "Once I stopped panicking about Matty, I started thinking. Remembering things the kinder had said." Without warning, Dorcas's voice trembled.

Sally put her hand over Dorcas's. "What about him? I've thought, a time or two, that he was paying a lot of attention to you."

Dorcas shrugged. "I've thought that, too. But it seems the kids' matchmaking has scared him off." She shook her head at a murmur of sympathy. "No, I'm all right."

"Sure?"

"I'll always be grateful for one thing. Thanks to Jacob, I know that it's possible to love again. That's a good outcome, even if not the best."

Sally squeezed her hand. "I think you're being too pessimistic. He has to have time to get used to the idea. Then…"

"It wouldn't work," Dorcas said quickly. "Think about it. The kinder, Sarry, my family… Our roots are here. I couldn't give up all that for the children. And his business, his life and Katie's life… They're all miles and miles away. It just wouldn't work. I have to accept it." She let out a long breath. "I have accepted it."

Sally studied her face. "I don't think so. Not yet."

"Maybe not, but soon. I have to. My children come first. They have only me."

* * *

As far as Jacob could see, the discussion with the bishop and other members of the church community had gone well. They understood the sort of work the prospective new machine shop would do, and as far as he could tell, no one objected to their limited use of computers for the necessary measuring.

He turned into Dorcas's lane with the rented buggy he'd been using. Reuben had stayed behind at the inn, working out some figures they'd need at tomorrow's meeting with Jackson, but he'd promised Katie she could drive him out on the road today. She wanted his enthusiastic agreement to her driving between the farm and town.

His thoughts scurried back to the reception of his business by the bishop and the others. How would it have gone if he hadn't had the backing of Abel and his family?

He'd been aware of all the interested glances going from him to Dorcas and back again, and he'd tried not to look at her. But he couldn't seem to help himself. He'd like to know what she felt about the children's matchmaking, but his face grew heated whenever he considered asking her.

He couldn't, not now when they were in the heat of the moment. It would be better when he'd returned home. A second marriage was something to be considered carefully and cautiously, especially when there were children involved.

Yes, going home tomorrow was the best solution. In his neat, quiet little house, with the business to occupy him, he could consider it from every angle.

He glanced toward the house and the

barn, trying to see if Katie was waiting for him, but the afternoon sun slanted through the trees, dazzling his eyes. In another moment he'd rounded the bend so that he could see the house. No Katie, but there was Matty running toward him, probably wanting a drive of his own.

Jacob started to smile, but then he had a closer look at the boy. That wasn't a look of welcome on his face. Matty looked frightened—no, terrified.

Whipping up the horse, he raced toward the boy, pulling up and jumping down when they were close to each other. Matty ran right into his arms, gasping for breath, tears staining his face.

Fear was contagious, and it raced through him. He held Matty, patting his back, trying to comfort him, trying to understand what was wrong.

"It's all right, Matty. Just tell me what's happening, so I can take care of it."

Matty stammered a few disconnected words and gasps, arms tight around Jacob's neck. He seemed unable to stop shaking and crying.

Jacob took hold of the boy's shoulders, holding him back so that he could see his face. "Matty! Komm, now. You have to tell me. Are you hurt?"

Matty shook his head. "Silas," he gasped. "Silas… He was trying to put a harness on his goat. He… I don't know what happened. I heard him cry, and then he fell down. He won't open his eyes or answer me or anything. Jacob…" He burst into sobs.

"Hush, now. You must run to the house for your mammi. You hear? Run fast as you can and tell her."

He was already rising to his feet. As Matty took off for the house, Jacob sprinted toward the barn, unspoken prayers rioting toward the heavens. *Please, Lord, please...*

Heart thudding, he tried to force his mind to work, but all it could do was cry out for help.

There, he could see the front of the barn—see the red wagon tipped over, see the goat grazing a few feet away. See the small figure crumpled in the dirt.

Silas... He skidded to a stop on his knees next to the boy. Silas, the thoughtful one, the one he knew least well. Quiet, but not this quiet.

Murmuring a prayer, he put his hand gently on Silas's chest, instantly reassured by his even breathing.

"Silas," he said softly. "Can you hear me?"

No response. Not even a flicker. His heart thudded against his chest wall. Silas had to be all right. He had to.

Quickly he ran his hands down the

boy's arms and legs, searching for injuries. Nothing. Then Silas's head—and he felt the lump rising even as he touched it. Fear clutched his heart. Concussion, brain injury…

Then Silas's eyelashes flickered.

"Silas," he said, heartened. "Open your eyes and look at me."

As if in response, Silas flickered his eyelids again and then opened his eyes. They were dazed, confused, but then they focused on Jacob's face.

"Jacob," he whispered and turned his face against Jacob's hand as if seeking support.

Breathing thanks, Jacob slid his arm under the boy's shoulders, drawing him close to his chest, feeling Silas's heart beating. His own heart seemed to be thudding in his ears…overflowing with love.

"It's all right now," he murmured.

"Mammi's coming. You're going to be fine."

Silas nestled against him. "Dumb goat," he muttered, surprising Jacob into a laugh.

"Not just the goat," he teased gently. "Next time you want to harness a goat, let me in on it first, yah?"

Silas's smile flickered. "Yah."

Then Dorcas was flying across the yard, face white. She fell to her knees next to them. "Ach, Silas, you're trying to scare us, yah?" Her eyes were terrified, but her voice was as calm as if he had dropped a fork. "You just lean on Jacob while I have a look at you."

She repeated what Jacob had done, running hands over him, checking for other injuries. Silas tried to pull himself up. He muttered, "Dizzy," and subsided.

"No wonder you're dizzy," Dorcas

said, voice husky. "You've got a great big lump on your head."

"It hurts." Now that his mother was there, his voice trembled, but he didn't let go of Jacob.

She cradled his face between her hands. "Not for long," she soothed, and the fear in her face was slipping away, but her eyes were still dark and frightened. "We'll put something cold on it."

"I'll carry him in." Jacob said it quickly, not wanting her to suggest that he go away.

Dorcas nodded, almost managing a smile.

Jacob rose, Silas cradled in his arms. He carried his precious burden toward the house, with Dorcas scurrying ahead.

By the time he reached the house, he had a feeling Silas was starting to enjoy all the attention. Katie and Sarry came running from upstairs with pillows and quilts, and Silas was established on the sofa and tucked in.

Then they ran to get a cold compress, both of them jostling each other to be first to reach the gas refrigerator.

Dorcas sat on the edge of the sofa, one hand on her son's cheek, the other reaching for Jacob's. Her gaze searched for answers, for reassurance, for comfort.

She needed him. Dorcas, who never showed that she needed anyone, needed him. And he…he loved her. All his questions were swept away in the clarity of that moment. He loved her.

"Do you think I should call the paramedics?" Her voice wobbled, and he could see that she was having second thoughts. She gripped his hand, her eyes pleading.

He folded her hand in both of his. "He seems more himself every minute.

Maybe just watch him a little longer. His eyes look normal, ain't so?"

She nodded. Her eyes brimmed with tears. With a quick gesture she pressed her cheek against his hand. "Denke," she whispered. "Denke."

Chapter Fifteen

Trying to keep Silas quiet for the next hour or so was more difficult than treating the lump on his head. Dorcas would no sooner settle him with a cold compress on his head than he'd reach for something and send the compress tumbling.

Dorcas was replacing it for the fourth time when Jacob came in with Timothy, who'd been helping James feed the herd and just gotten back.

"I told Timothy about Silas and the goat," Jacob said, keeping his tone light and giving her a cautioning look. "You have something he can do to help, ain't so?"

She got the message that underlay his words. Timothy would benefit most from doing something useful at this point, probably because he felt bad at not being here for his little brother.

"Sure thing." She put a hand on Timothy's shoulder and drew him closer to her. "Silas needs to be still and keep a compress on his head until the bump goes down. Maybe if you could find a quiet game to play or a story to read, that would do the trick."

Timothy was already nodding vigorously. "Yah, sure, Mammi. I'll take care of it. Maybe if we tie something soft over the compress, too. I'll see to it."

He rushed off to the living room, the door swinging, and she soon could hear the soft murmur of voices, punctuated by the click of checkers.

Dorcas turned to Jacob. "Denke. It was good of you to tell him. I'm sure he was upset."

"Feeling guilty," he said. "We're all feeling guilty."

She started to shake her head, but he went on quickly. "Don't deny it. You were blaming yourself for not being in two places at once. Timothy blames himself because just yesterday he promised that he'd look out for the younger ones."

He'd seen right through her and Timothy, that was certain sure. He was right, but she was stung at his words. What about himself?

"And you? What do you feel guilty about?"

She was sorry the instant the words were out, but it was too late. Jacob's face tightened until it resembled a stone. He looked now the way he had that first day when he'd shown up chasing Katie.

Only now she knew what was beneath the stone—a man who had a warm heart but also an iron fence preventing him from showing it.

She didn't expect him to answer, and the silence drew out between them—tense and prickly. Suddenly he grimaced, as if his face reflected a sharp inner pain.

"Guilt?" He spat out the word. "I'm guilty because I've been living a lie for years. A lie that's affected everything I've done and said since Teresa died."

It was a wonder that her mouth wasn't hanging open, Dorcas told herself. She'd known there was something, but…

"Ach, I know. You thought I'd never shown an interest in another woman because I was still grieving my dead wife."

Jacob turned, took two long steps toward the door, and then turned again and came back. He grabbed the edge of the kitchen counter as if to anchor himself.

"Your wife…" Dorcas ventured. "Everyone says she died in an accident. You can't feel guilty about an accident."

"It was an accident, yah." He stared down at the counter without seeming to see it. "They don't say, because they don't know, what she was doing when the accident took place. Teresa was leaving me. Running away because she couldn't stand living with me any longer."

His mouth clamped shut. He held tight to the counter, and it seemed his whole taut body was a cry of pain. Dorcas struggled to find her way through the chaos in her mind.

Jacob was in tremendous pain, that much was clear. Was it better to leave him alone? Or to encourage him to speak—to say the rest of it?

As soon as she framed the questions, Dorcas knew the answer. Now that he'd let out some part of what he'd been hiding, he needed to say the rest of it. How else could he possibly find peace?

Gently, tentatively, she spoke, praying no one would come in and interrupt. "How did you know that? Did she tell you?"

"I should have sensed it," he muttered. "Any man should realize something like that about his own wife. But I didn't. I was so caught up in my business that I didn't see her loneliness. I didn't see that our marriage wasn't enough. Not until I came home and found her gone and read the note she left."

"I'm sorry," she murmured. "But why? Why doesn't anyone know the truth?"

"She died," he said bleakly. "The news

of the accident came through before I could do anything. Her family was devastated. All anyone knew was that it was an accident." He turned toward her almost as if he was blaming her, but she knew it was himself he blamed. "What could I do? Make everything worse by telling them that she'd broken her vows and deserted me?"

She didn't know what the church would say, but she knew that if she were in his position, she'd have done the same thing he did.

Forcing herself to move, Dorcas put her hand on his arm. It felt like an iron bar under her fingers, and she tried to send caring through her touch.

"There was nothing else you could do. You spared them more pain. That shouldn't make you feel guilty."

He shook his head. "Not that, no. I'm guilty because I was so busy that I didn't know enough about my own wife. So I just lived with that…until I met you." He turned, and now he clasped both her hands. "Ach, Dorcas, I had to tell you the truth. I couldn't let myself say I love you unless you knew the truth."

Dorcas could only look at him, hardly able to believe what he'd just said. Love. He loved her.

Jacob pressed her hands against his chest, and she could feel his heart thumping. Her own was probably beating just as fast. She couldn't say she hadn't been thinking about this, even hoping for it. But now that it had happened, she was hardly able to believe in it.

"Jacob…are you sure?"

His eyes warmed, and he gave a low laugh. "Do you think I go around proposing to women if I'm not sure?"

"That was…you want to marry me?"

"If you think you can take a chance on me. I didn't do so well the first time."

"You were a boy then." The words came out without thought. "You and Teresa... It sounds as if neither of you was ready for marriage." Her heart thudded, almost keeping her from speaking. "Are you ready now?"

"Yah, I am. And you will marry me, won't you, Dorcas? I didn't realize... didn't even consider the possibility until suddenly I looked at you and knew I loved you."

He lifted a hand and touched her cheek caressingly. "Marry me, Dorcas. I want to take care of you. And the children, of course. My house won't be big enough for us, but I'll find a place outside of Bellville, not too far from the business."

Bellville... She repeated the word in her mind. Jacob expected they would marry and live in Bellville, far away from the rest of her family. How could she take the children away from everything they knew? From all the people who loved them?

"I… Jacob, we need to think about this. It's not so simple. I'm responsible for the children. I can't decide all at once."

Slowly the happiness faded from his face. He took a step back, no longer touching her. "If you mean no…"

The door burst open, admitting Matty followed by Katie and then Sarry. Dorcas bit her lip. Why did they come in now?

"Where is everybody?" Matty declared. "We did all the chores. Sarry said we should take care of them, so we did. Is Silas sleeping?"

"Not with you shouting," Katie said, pulling him back against her. She was looking from Jacob to Dorcas, obviously wondering what was happening. "Did we interrupt? Should we go out again?"

"No need." Jacob's voice was flat, and he moved quickly to the door. "I have to get ready for the meeting tomorrow. Goodnight, everyone."

How could he leave now? She wanted to shout at him. Did he want to marry her or not? Didn't he understand that there was much to consider? Was he trying to rush into marriage with her the way he apparently had with Teresa?

With an effort she shut the door of her mind on the thought of what had just happened. She felt as if she'd been whirling on one of those rides she'd seen at the fair. Now it was time to get off.

Jacob had to understand that she couldn't undertake any life-changing decision without a lot of consideration. She wasn't a twenty-year-old without a responsibility in the world.

She was a woman with three children, a sister to care for, people she loved. If Jacob couldn't understand that, then this glimpse of happiness was nothing more than that—just a glimpse.

Jacob splashed cold water on his face before going downstairs at the inn the next morning. He and Reuben would leave to make an offer on the property shortly, and he tried to stay focused on the meeting. He needed to have all his wits about him, and he couldn't do that if he let himself go back to reliving everything that had happened with Dorcas the previous day.

Reuben was waiting for him on the porch of the inn, his small bag at his feet, since the plan was to head back to Bellville after the meeting. He'd managed to forget that. His bag, not even packed, lay upstairs on his bed. How could he deal with business when he couldn't even remember to pack his bag?

"Aren't you planning to go back with me today?" Reuben gave him a questioning look.

"I don't… I haven't decided yet. I may need to speak to Dorcas again. About Katie," he added quickly.

Reuben seemed to suppress a smile. "Will you tell her I enjoyed meeting her?" He hesitated, then went on, looking down the road as if watching for Charlie with the car. "She's a fine woman, anyone can see. Devoted to her family."

Fine, now even Reuben was getting involved with his private life. Everyone seemed to know what he should be doing. Everyone but himself.

"Yah," he said shortly. Devoted to her family, that was true. So devoted that she'd say no to marriage with him in order to keep them happy?

He hadn't put it in those words, not even to himself. He tried to think about everything he'd said, everything she'd said, in that conversation in the kitchen. A conversation that was interrupted, as always, by the family.

Charlie's car was coming down the block. He had to concentrate on business, but he couldn't.

Interrupted? That was what he kept saying. Kept complaining, but was that true? Or had he been alone so long that he'd forgotten what family meant?

The car pulled up and stopped. Reuben took several steps toward it and looked back at him. "Jacob?"

Jacob glanced down at the case that held all the papers they'd been working on. Business. Always business. Important, but not more important than everything else.

He thrust the case into Reuben's hands,

almost laughing at Reuben's expression. "Here," he said. "You go on and deal with this."

"But..."

"It's time you came in as a partner. You know as much about the business as I do, ain't so? Your first job as partner is to go ahead and make the deal. I have something more important to take care of."

Reuben looked stunned for another moment. Then his face broke into a smile. "Yah, you do," he said.

Charlie was leaning across the seat, an interested observer, and he began to chuckle. "You want us to drop you off first?"

"No, thanks." He was probably looking like a grinning clown, but he didn't care. "I'll do my courting the right way...in a courting buggy."

Sent on his way by their laughter, he

rounded the side of the inn and headed for the stable. This had to be taken care of first. Family was more important than business. That was the mistake he'd been making all along. Family wasn't an interruption. It was life.

Even the buggy mare seemed to get into the spirit this morning, trotting along the familiar road, head high. They must have made record time getting to Dorcas's house.

It was so early the boys wouldn't have gone to school yet. The family would probably still be at breakfast or doing morning chores. Good, that was the way he wanted it.

Riding on a wave of enthusiasm, he jumped down and tossed the lines over the hitching rail. Timothy and Silas appeared from the barn and Matty from the chicken coop. In an instant they were running toward him. He waited, knowing that everyone had to be there.

As they swarmed up to him, chattering, asking why he was back this morning and was he going to stay, he shooed them toward the kitchen.

"Hurry. I need to talk to everyone." They rushed inside. To his relief, Dorcas and Katie and Sarry were all there, looking at him with varying degrees of surprise.

"We thought you had an important meeting this morning." Dorcas said the words as if asking a question.

"Reuben is taking care of that. I have something more important to do."

He hoped she understood the meaning of what he was telling her. That business wasn't as important as family. After all, she had said it to him, first.

A slow smile warmed her face. "What could be more important than business?"

"Family." He looked around the circle of faces. "I want to get married and have a family, so I'm asking you. All of you. Sarry, Katie, Timothy, Silas, Matty…even that foolish goat and this place. I want all of you. You all come with Mammi, ain't so?"

For an instant the kitchen was as silent as he'd once wanted it. Then Matty flung himself against Jacob's leg and clung tight. Silas, careful of his tender forehead, pressed against his arm. Timothy met his gaze steadily for a moment. As if a question had been answered, he pressed against Jacob's other arm. Katie and Sarry threw themselves into the hug, laughing.

Over their heads, Jacob met Dorcas's gaze. She was smiling, and he thought she'd never looked more beautiful. She came closer, peeling her way through the group until she could reach up and take his face in her hands.

The doubts and questions were all swept away. It wouldn't be easy, for sure. Family life was never meant to be easy.

I'll do my best for your children, he thought, thinking of the man he'd never met.

And then Dorcas drew his head down. His lips met hers, and their kiss sealed the promise. They were family.

Later, when the boys had gone off to school, complaining about having to go on such an important day, and Katie and Sarry had found something to keep them busy in the kitchen, Dorcas sat down next to Jacob in the porch swing.

He put his arm around her, and she slid closer to him. "Are you still sure?" she asked, loving the way his eyes crinkled at the question.

"I'm wonderful sure," he said. "I have what I've been missing most of my life."

"Sure you're not going to miss the business?" Her one fear was that after life settled down here, he'd find he longed to be back in Bellville.

"What is there to miss? When I finally started thinking about it, I realized the answer was there all along. Reuben deserves to be a partner, and he'll take care of everything in Bellville. And I'll have the fun of starting a new machine shop here, where my family is."

Dorcas could feel his certainty warming her heart. She leaned her head against his shoulder, loving the sensation of his strong arm around her. "I was just thinking about the day we found Katie in the barn. I certainly didn't imagine what that was going to lead to."

Jacob pressed a kiss against her forehead. "You know, it seems to me that everything… Katie's running away, the children's matchmaking, Silas's accident, all those things must have been part of God's plan. God was ready to bring us together into a new family."

She looked up into his serious, loving face. "It won't always be easy, but with God's help, we can do it."

"Yah," he said, and he kissed her again.

"Dorcas!" The shrill voice had them pulling apart as if they were guilty teenagers. Aunt Lizzie was there in the lane, almost falling out of her buggy as she stared at them. "What are you doing?"

Before she could answer, she felt Jacob's arm drawing her close again.

"You are just in time to be the first to know. Dorcas and I are going to be married. Can I call you Aunt Lizzie?"

Dorcas nearly dissolved in helpless giggles, but she just managed to control herself.

Aunt Lizzie looked from Jacob's face to hers. "Is this true, Dorcas?"

All she could manage was to nod, but that seemed to be enough.

"Well!" Aunt Lizzie began, and Dorcas braced herself for the storm. "If that's so, young man, you can come and take the horse for me." She started to get down, and Jacob hurried to help her.

Collecting herself, Dorcas pulled the door open. She'd best make sure the remains of their morning celebration were cleared up and put some coffee on.

As the door swung behind her, she heard one more comment from Aunt Lizzie. "I guess you had better call me Aunt Lizzie."

She escaped, giggling helplessly, into the house. She wondered if Jacob was thinking what she was… That if he'd won over Aunt Lizzie, there would be nothing to worry about with the rest of the community. Everyone would be celebrating with them.

"Thank You, Lord," she said softly. "Thank You."

* * * * *

If you enjoyed this story,
don't miss the previous books in the
Brides of Lost Creek series from
Marta Perry:

Second Chance Amish Bride
The Wedding Quilt Bride
The Promised Amish Bride
The Amish Widow's Heart
A Secret Amish Crush
Nursing Her Amish Neighbor

Dear Reader,

I'm so glad to be back in Lost Creek again. I feel as if I'm walking the familiar streets and driving past the farms, stopping at a quilt shop and enjoying a Mud Sale. Best of all, I have caught up with a number of characters I know from earlier books!

I hope you'll enjoy reading this story as much as I enjoyed writing it. It's good to know that love can come again after loss and that people who've given up on love can be surprised by God in a whole new way.

I hope you'll let me know if you enjoyed it by emailing me at mpjohn@ptd.net. I'd love to hear from you.

Blessings,
Marta Perry